The Woman in Black

THE
WOMAN IN BLACK

A Ghost Story by SUSAN HILL

Illustrations by John Lawrence

DAVID R. GODINE
Publisher · Boston

For Pat and Charles Gardner

First U.S. edition published in 1986 by
DAVID R. GODINE · *Publisher*
Post Office Box 450
Jaffrey, New Hampshire 03452
www.godine.com

Originally published in the U.K. in 1983
by Hamish Hamilton Ltd.

Library of Congress Cataloging-in-Publication Data
Hill, Susan, 1942–
The woman in black.
1. Title.
PR6058.145w6 1985 823'.914 85-70145
ISBN 1-56792-189-2 (SC)

Fifth softcover printing 2010
PRINTED IN THE UNITED STATES OF AMERICA

Contents

CHRISTMAS EVE

IT WAS NINE-THIRTY on Christmas Eve. As I crossed the long entrance hall of Monk's Piece on my way from the dining room, where we had just enjoyed the first of the happy, festive meals, towards the drawing room and the fire around which my family were now assembled, I paused and then, as I often do in the course of an evening, went to the front door, opened it and stepped outside.

I have always liked to take a breath of the evening, to smell the air, whether it is sweetly scented and balmy with the flowers of mid-summer, pungent with the bonfires and leafmould of autumn, or crackling cold from frost and snow. I like to look about me at the sky above my head, whether there are moon and stars or utter black-ness, and into the darkness ahead of me; I like to listen for the cries of nocturnal creatures and the moaning rise and fall of the wind, or the pattering of rain in the orchard trees, I enjoy the rush of air towards me up the hill from the flat pastures of the river valley.

Tonight, I smelled at once, and with a lightening heart, that there had been a change in the weather. All the previous week, we had had rain, thin, chilling rain and a mist that lay low about the house and over the countryside. From the windows, the view stretched no farther than a yard or two down the garden. It was wretched weather, never seeming to come fully light, and raw, too. There had been no pleasure in walking, the visibility was too poor for any shooting and the dogs were permanently morose and muddy. Inside the house, the lamps were lit throughout the day and the walls of larder, outhouse and cellar oozed damp and smelled sour, the fires sputtered and smoked, burning dismally low.

My spirits have for many years now been excessively affected by the ways of the weather, and I confess that, had it not been for the air of cheerfulness and bustle that prevailed in the rest of the house, I should have been quite cast down in gloom and lethargy, unable to enjoy the flavour of life as I should like and irritated by my own susceptibility. But Esmé is merely stung by inclement weather into a spirited defiance, and so the preparations for our Christmas holiday had this year been more than usually extensive and vigorous.

I took a step or two out from under the shadow of the house so that I could see around me in the moonlight. Monk's Piece stands at the summit of land that rises gently up for some four hundred feet from where the little River Nee traces its winding way in a north to south direction across this fertile, and sheltered, part of the country. Below us are pastures, interspersed with small clumps of mixed, broadleaf woodland. But at our backs for several square miles it is a quite different area of rough scrub and heathland, a patch of wildness in the midst of well-farmed country. We are but two miles from a good-sized village, seven from the principal market town, yet there is an air of remoteness and isolation which makes us feel ourselves to be much further from civilisation.

I first saw Monk's Piece one afternoon in high summer, when out driving in the trap with Mr Bentley. Mr Bentley was formerly my employer, but I had lately risen to become a full partner in the firm of lawyers to which I had been articled as a young man (and with whom, indeed, I remained for my entire working life). He was at this time nearing the age when he had begun to feel inclined to let slip the reins of responsibility, little by little, from his own hands into mine, though he continued to travel up to our chambers in London at least once a week, until he died in his eighty-second year. But he was becoming more and more of a country-dweller. He was no man for shooting and fishing but, instead, he had immersed himself in the roles of country magistrate and churchwarden, governor of this, that and the other county and parish board, body and committee. I had been both relieved and pleased when finally he took me into full partnership with himself, after so many years, while at the same time believing the position to be no more than my due, for I had done my fair share of the donkey work and borne a good deal of the burden of responsibility for directing the fortunes of the firm with, I felt, inadequate reward — at least in terms of position.

So it came about that I was sitting beside Mr Bentley on a Sunday afternoon, enjoying the view over the high hawthorn hedgerows across the green, drowsy countryside, as he let his pony take the road back, at a gentle pace, to his somewhat ugly and over-imposing manor house. It was rare for me to sit back and do nothing. In London I lived for my work, apart from some spare time spent in the study and collecting of watercolours. I was then thirty-five and I had been a widower for the past twelve years. I had no taste at all for social life and, although in good general health, was prone to occasional nervous illnesses and conditions, as a result of the experiences I will come to relate. Truth to tell, I was growing old well before my time, a sombre, pale-complexioned man with a strained expression — a dull dog.

I remarked to Mr Bentley on the calm and sweetness of the day, and after a sideways glance in my direction he said, 'You should think of getting yourself something in this direction — why not? Pretty little cottage — down there, perhaps?' And he pointed with his whip to where a tiny hamlet was tucked snugly into a bend of the river below, white walls basking in the afternoon sunshine. 'Bring yourself out of town some of these Friday afternoons, take to walking, fill yourself up with fresh air and good eggs and cream.'

The idea had a charm, but only a distant one, seemingly unrelated to myself, and so I merely smiled and breathed in the warm

3

scents of the grasses and the field flowers and watched the dust kicked up off the lane by the pony's hooves and thought no more about it. Until, that is, we reached a stretch of road leading past a long, perfectly proportioned stone house, set on a rise above a sweeping view down over the whole river valley and then for miles away to the violet-blue line of hills in the distance.

At that moment, I was seized by something I cannot precisely describe, an emotion, a desire — no, it was rather more, a knowledge, a simple *certainty*, which gripped me, and all so clear and striking that I cried out involuntarily for Mr Bentley to stop, and, almost before he had time to do so climbed out of the pony trap into the lane and stood on a grassy knoll, gazing first up at the house, so handsome, so utterly right for the position it occupied, a modest house and yet sure of itself, and then looking across at the country beyond. I had no sense of having been here before, but an absolute conviction that I would come here again, that the house was already mine, bound to me invisibly.

To one side of it, a stream ran between the banks towards the meadow beyond, whence it made its meandering way down to the river.

Mr Bentley was now looking at me curiously, from the trap. 'A fine place,' he called.

I nodded, but, quite unable to impart to him any of my extreme emotions, turned my back upon him and walked a few yards up the slope from where I could see the entrance to the old, overgrown orchard that lay behind the house and petered out in long grass and tangled thicket at the far end. Beyond that, I glimpsed the perimeter of some rough-looking, open land. The feeling of conviction I have described was still upon me, and I remember that I was alarmed by it, for I had never been an imaginative or fanciful man and certainly not one given to visions of the future. Indeed, since those earlier experiences I had deliberately avoided all contemplation of any remotely nonmaterial matters, and clung to the prosaic, the visible and tangible.

Nevertheless, I was quite unable to escape the belief — nay, I must call it more, the certain knowledge — that this house was one day to be my own home, that sooner or later, though I had no idea when, I would become the owner of it. When finally I accepted and admitted this to myself, I felt on that instant a profound sense of peace and contentment settle upon me such as I had not known for very many years, and it was with a light heart that I returned to the pony trap, where Mr Bentley was awaiting me more than a little curiously.

The overwhelming feeling I had experienced at Monk's Piece remained with me, albeit not in the forefront of my mind, when I left the country that afternoon to return to London. I had told Mr Bentley that if ever he were to hear that the house was for sale, I should be eager to know of it.

Some years later, he did so. I contacted the agents that same day and hours later, without so much as returning to see it again, I had offered for it, and my offer was accepted. A few months prior to this, I had met Esmé Ainley. Our affection for one another had been increasing steadily, but, cursed as I still was by my indecisive nature in all personal and emotional matters, I had remained silent as to my intentions for the future. I had enough sense to take the news about Monk's Piece as a good omen, however, and a week after I had formally become the owner of the house, travelled into the country with Esmé and proposed marriage to her among the trees of the old orchard. This offer, too, was accepted and very shortly afterwards we were married and moved at once to Monk's Piece. On that day, I truly believed that I had at last come out from under the long shadow cast by the events of the past and saw from his face and felt from the warmth of his handclasp that Mr Bentley believed it too, and that a burden had been lifted from his own shoulders. He had always blamed himself, at least in part, for what had happened to me — it had, after all, been he who had sent me on that first journey up to Crythin Gifford, and Eel Marsh House, and to the funeral of Mrs Drablow.

But all of that could not have been further from my conscious thought at least, as I stood taking in the night air at the door of my house, on that Christmas Eve. For some fourteen years now Monk's Piece had been the happiest of homes — Esmé's and mine, and that of her four children by her first marriage, to Captain Ainley. In the early days I had come here only at weekends and holidays, but London life and business began to irk me from the day I bought the place and I was glad indeed to retire permanently into the country at the earliest opportunity.

And, now, it was to this happy home that my family had once again repaired for Christmas. In a moment, I should open the front door and hear the sound of their voices from the drawing room unless I was abruptly summoned by my wife, fussing about my catching a chill. Certainly, it was very cold and clear at last. The sky was pricked over with stars and the full moon rimmed with a halo of frost. The dampness and fogs of the past week had stolen away like thieves into the night, the paths and the stone walls of the house gleamed palely and my breath smoked on the air.

Upstairs, in the attic bedrooms, Isobel's three young sons — Esmé's grandsons — slept, with stockings tied to their bedposts. There would be no snow for them on the morrow, but Christmas Day would at least wear a bright and cheerful countenance.

There was something in the air that night, something, I suppose, remembered from my own happy childhood, together with an infection caught from the little boys, that excited me, old as I was. That my peace of mind was about to be disturbed, and memories awakened that I had thought forever dead, I had, naturally, no idea.

That I should ever again renew my close acquaintance, if only in the course of vivid recollections and dreams, with mortal dread and terror of spirit, would have seemed at that moment impossible.

I took one last look at the frosty darkness, sighed contentedly, called to the dogs, and went in, anticipating nothing more than a pipe and a glass of good malt whisky beside the crackling fire, in the happy company of my family. As I crossed the hall and entered the drawing room, I felt an uprush of well-being, of the kind I have experienced regularly during my life at Monk's Piece, a sensation that leads on naturally to another, of heartfelt thankfulness. And indeed I did give thanks, at the sight of my family ensconced around the huge fire which Oliver was at that moment building to a perilous height and a fierce blaze with the addition of a further great branch of applewood from an old tree we had felled in the orchard the previous autumn. Oliver is the eldest of Esmé's sons, and bore then, as now, a close resemblance both to his sister Isobel (seated beside her husband, the bearded Aubrey Pearce) and to the brother next in age, Will. All three of them have good, plain, open English faces, inclined to roundness and with hair and eyebrows and lashes of a light chestnut brown the colour of their mother's hair before it became threaded with grey.

At that time, Isobel was only twenty-four years old but already the mother of three young sons, and set fair to produce more. She had the plump, settled air of a matron and an inclination to mother and oversee her husband and brothers as well as her own children. She had been the most sensible, responsible of daughters, she was affectionate and charming, and she seemed to have found, in the calm and level-headed Aubrey Pearce, an ideal partner. Yet at times I caught Esmé looking at her wistfully, and she had more than once voiced, though gently and to me alone, a longing for Isobel to be a little less staid, a little more spirited, even frivolous.

In all honesty, I could not have wished it so. I would not have wished for anything to ruffle the surface of that calm, untroubled sea.

Oliver Ainley, at that time nineteen, and his brother Will, only fourteen months younger, were similarly serious, sober young men at heart, but for the time being they still enjoyed all the exuberance of young puppies, and indeed it seemed to me that Oliver showed rather too few signs of maturity for a young man in his first year at Cambridge and destined, if my advice prevailed with him, for a career at the Bar. Will lay on his stomach before the fire, his face aglow, chin propped upon his hands. Oliver sat nearby, and from time to time a scuffle of their long legs would break out, a kicking and shoving, accompanied by a sudden guffawing, for all the world as if they were ten years old all over again.

The youngest of the Ainleys, Edmund, sat a little apart, separating himself, as was his wont, a little distance from every other person, not out of any unfriendliness or sullen temper but because of an innate fastidiousness and reserve, a desire to be somewhat private, which had always singled him out from the rest of Esmé's family, just as he was also unlike the others in looks, being pale-skinned, and long-nosed, with hair of an extraordinary blackness, and blue eyes. Edmund was then fifteen. I knew him the least well, understood him scarcely at all, felt uneasy in his presence, and yet perhaps in a strange way loved him more deeply than any.

The drawing room at Monk's Piece is long and low, with tall windows at either end, close-curtained now, but by day letting in a great deal of light from both north and south. Tonight, festoons and swags of fresh greenery, gathered that afternoon by Esmé and Isobel, hung over the stone fireplace, and intertwined with the leaves were berries and ribbons of scarlet and gold. At the far end of the room stood the tree, candlelit and bedecked, and beneath it were piled the presents. There were flowers, too, vases of white chrysanthemums, and in the centre of the room, on a round table, a pyramid of gilded fruit and a bowl of oranges stuck all about with cloves, their spicy scent filling the air and mingling with that of the branches and the wood smoke to be the very aroma of Christmas.

I sat down in my own armchair, drew it back a little from the full blaze of the fire, and began the protracted and soothing business of lighting a pipe. As I did so, I became aware that I had interrupted the others in the midst of a lively conversation, and that Oliver and Will at least were restless to continue.

'Well,' I said, through the first, cautious puffs at my tobacco, 'and what's all this?'

8

There was a further pause, and Esmé shook her head, smiling, over her embroidery.

'Come. . .'

Then Oliver got to his feet and began to go about the room rapidly switching off every lamp, save the lights upon the Christmas tree at the far end, so that, when he returned to his seat, we had only the immediate firelight by which to see one another, and Esmé was obliged to lay down her sewing — not without a murmur of protest.

'May as well do the job properly,' Oliver said with some satisfaction.

'Oh, you boys. . .'

'Now come on, Will, your turn, isn't it?'

'No, Edmund's.'

'Ah-ha,' said the youngest of the Ainley brothers, in an odd, deep voice. 'I could an' if I would!'

'*Must* we have the lights out?' Isobel spoke as if to much smaller boys.

'Yes, Sis, we must, that's if you want to get the authentic atmosphere.'

'But I'm not sure that I do.'

Oliver gave a low moan. 'Get on with it then, someone.'

Esmé leaned over towards me. 'They are telling ghost stories.'

'Yes,' said Will, his voice unsteady with both excitement and laughter. 'Just the thing for Christmas Eve. It's an ancient tradition!'

'The lonely country house, the guests huddled around the fireside in a darkened room, the wind howling at the casement. . .' Oliver moaned again.

And then came Aubrey's stolid, good-humoured tones. 'Better get on with it then.' And so they did, Oliver, Edmund and Will vying with one another to tell the horridest, most spine-chilling tale, with much dramatic effect and mock-terrified shrieking. They outdid one another in the far extremes of inventiveness, piling agony upon agony. They told of dripping stone walls in uninhabited castles and of ivy-clad monastery ruins by moonlight, of locked inner rooms and secret dungeons, dank charnel houses and overgrown graveyards, of footsteps creaking upon staircases and fingers tapping at casements, of howlings and shriekings, groanings and scuttlings and the clanking of chains, of hooded monks and headless horsemen, swirling mists and sudden winds, insubstantial spectres and sheeted creatures, vampires and bloodhounds, bats and rats and spiders, of men found at dawn and women turned white-haired and raving lunatic, and of vanished corpses and curses upon heirs. The stories grew more and more lurid, wilder and sillier, and soon the gasps and cries merged into fits of choking laughter, as each one, even gentle Isobel, contributed more ghastly detail.

At first, I was amused, indulgent, but as I sat on, listening, in the firelight, I began to feel set apart from them all, an outsider to their circle. I was trying to suppress my mounting unease, to hold back the rising flood of memory.

This was a sport, a high-spirited and harmless game among young people, for the festive season, and an ancient tradition, too, as Will had rightly said; there was nothing to torment and trouble me, nothing of which I could possibly disapprove. I did not want to seem a killjoy, old and stodgy and unimaginative, I longed to enter into what was nothing more nor less than good fun. I fought a bitter battle within myself, my head turned away from the fire-light so that none of them should chance to see my expression which I knew began to show signs of my discomfiture.

And then, to accompany a final, banshee howl from Edmund, the log that had been blazing on the hearth collapsed suddenly and, after sending up a light spatter of sparks and ash, died down so that there was near-darkness. And then silence in the room. I shud-dered. I wanted to get up and go round putting on every light again, see the sparkle and glitter and colour of the Christmas dec-orations, have the fire blazing again cheerfully; I wanted to banish the chill that had settled upon me and the sensation of fear in my breast. Yet I could not move; it had, for the moment, paralysed me, just as it had always done, it was a long-forgotten, once too-famil-iar sensation.

Then, Edmund said, 'Now come, Stepfather, your turn,' and at once the others took up the cry, the silence was broken by their urgings, with which even Esmé joined.

'No, no.' I tried to speak jocularly. 'Nothing from me.'

'Oh, Arthur. . .'

'You must know at least *one* ghost story, Stepfather, everyone knows *one*. . .'

Ah, yes, yes, indeed. All the time I had been listening to their ghoulish, lurid inventions, and their howlings and groans, the one thought that had been in my mind, and the only thing I could have said was, 'No, no, you have none of you any idea. This is all nonsense, fantasy, it is not like this. Nothing so blood-curdling and becreepered and crude — not so . . . so laughable. The truth is quite other, and altogether more terrible.'

'Come on, Stepfather.'

'Don't be an old spoilsport.'

'Arthur?'

'Do your stuff, Stepfather, surely you're not going to let us down?'

I stood up, unable to bear it any longer.

'I am sorry to disappoint you,' I said. 'But I have no story to tell!' And went quickly from the room, and from the house.

Some fifteen minutes later, I came to my senses and found myself on the scrubland beyond the orchard, my heart pounding, my breathing short. I had walked about in a frenzy of agitation, and now, realising that I must make an effort to calm myself, I sat down on a piece of old, moss-covered stone, and began to take deliberate, steady breaths in on a count of ten and out again, until I felt the tension within myself begin to slacken and my pulse become a little steadier, my head clearer. After a short while longer, I was able to realise my surroundings once again, to note the clearness of the sky and the brightness of the stars, the air's coldness and the crispiness of the frost-stiffened grass beneath my feet.

Behind me, in the house, I knew that I must have left the family in a state of consternation and bewilderment, for they knew me normally as an even-tempered man of predictable emotions. Why they had aroused my apparent disapproval with the telling of a few silly tales and prompted such curt behaviour, the whole family would be quite at a loss to understand, and very soon I must return to them, make amends and endeavour to brush off the incident, renew some of the air of jollity. What I would not be able to do was explain. No. I would be cheerful and I would be steady again, if only for my dear wife's sake, but no more.

They had chided me with being a spoilsport, tried to encourage me to tell them the one ghost story I must surely, like any other man, have it in me to tell. And they were right. Yes, I had a story, a true story, a story of haunting and evil, fear and confusion, horror and tragedy. But it was not a story to be told for casual entertainment, around the fireside upon Christmas Eve.

I had always known in my heart that the experience would never leave me, that it was now woven into my very fibres, an inextricable part of my past, but I had hoped never to have to recollect it, consciously, and in full, ever again. Like an old wound, it gave off a faint twinge now and again, but less and less often, less and less painfully, as the years went on and my happiness, sanity and equilibrium were assured. Of late, it had been like the outermost ripple on a pool, merely the faint memory of a memory.

Now, tonight, it again filled my mind to the exclusion of all else. I knew that I should have no rest from it, that I should lie awake in a chill of sweat, going over that time, those events, those places. So it had been night after night for years.

I got up and began to walk about again. Tomorrow was Christmas Day. Could I not be free of it at least for that blessed time, was there no way of keeping the memory, and the effects it had upon me, at bay, as an analgesic or a balm will stave off the pain of a wound, at least temporarily? And then, standing among the trunks of the fruit trees, silver-gray in the moonlight, I recalled that the way to banish an old ghost that continues its hauntings is to exorcise it. Well then, mine should be exorcised. I should tell my tale, not aloud, by the fireside, not as a diversion for idle listeners — it was too solemn, and too real, for that. But I should set it down on paper, with every care and in every detail. I would write my own ghost story. Then perhaps I should finally be free of it for whatever life remained for me to enjoy.

I decided at once that it should be, at least during my lifetime, a story for my eyes only. I was the one who had been haunted and who had suffered — not the only one, no, but surely, I thought, the only one left alive, I was the one who, to judge by my agitation of this evening, was still affected by it deeply — it was from me alone that the ghost must be driven.

I glanced up at the moon, and at the bright, bright polestar. Christmas Eve. And then I prayed, a heartfelt, simple prayer for peace of mind, and for strength and steadfastness to endure while I completed what would be the most agonising task, and I prayed for a blessing upon my family, and for quiet rest to us all that night. For, although I was in control of my emotions now, I dreaded the hours of darkness that lay ahead.

For answer to my prayer, I received immediately the memory of some lines of poetry, lines I had once known but long forgotten. Later, I spoke them aloud to Esmé, and she identified the source for me at once.

> 'Some say that ever 'gainst that season comes
> Wherein our Saviour's birth is celebrated,
> This bird of dawning singeth all night long.
> And then, they say, no spirit dare stir abroad,
> The nights are wholesome, then no planets strike,
> No Fairy takes, nor witch hath power to charm,
> So hallowed and so gracious is that time.'

As I recited them aloud, a great peace came upon me, I was wholly myself again yet stiffened by my resolution. After this holiday, when the family had all departed, and Esmé and I were alone, I would begin to write my story.

When I returned to the house, Isobel and Aubrey had gone upstairs to share the delight of creeping about with bulging stockings for their young sons, Edmund was reading, Oliver and Will were in the old playroom at the far end of the house, where there was a battered billiard table, and Esmé was tidying the drawing room, preparatory to going to bed. About that evening's incident, nothing whatsoever was said, though she wore an anxious expression, and I had to invent a bad bout of acute indigestion to account for my abrupt behaviour. I saw to the fire, damping down the flames, and knocked out my pipe on the side of the hearth, feeling quiet and serene again, and no longer agitated about what lonely terrors I might have to endure, whether asleep or awake, during the small hours of the coming night.

Tomorrow was Christmas Day, and I looked forward to it eagerly and with gladness. It would be a time of family joy and merrymaking, love and friendship, fun and laughter.

When it was over, I would have work to do.

A LONDON PARTICULAR

I T WAS A MONDAY afternoon in November and already growing dark, not because of the lateness of the hour — it was barely three o'clock — but because of the fog, the thickest of London
pea-soupers, which had hemmed us in on all sides since dawn —
if, indeed, there had been a dawn, for the fog had scarcely allowed
any daylight to penetrate the foul gloom of the atmosphere.

Fog was outdoors, hanging over the river, creeping in and out
of alleyways and passages, swirling thickly between the bare trees
of all the parks and gardens of the city, and indoors, too, seething
through cracks and crannies like sour breath, gaining a sly entrance
at every opening of a door. It was a yellow fog, a filthy, evil-smelling
fog, a fog that choked and blinded, smeared and stained. Groping
their way blindly across roads, men and women took their lives in
their hands, stumbling along the pavements, they clutched at railings and at one another, for guidance.

Sounds were deadened, shapes blurred. It was a fog that had
come three days before, and did not seem inclined to go away and
it had, I suppose, the quality of all such fogs — it was menacing

and sinister, disguising the familiar world and confusing the people in it, as they were confused by having their eyes covered and being turned about, in a game of blindman's buff.

It was, in all, miserable weather and lowering to the spirits in the drearest month of the year.

It would be easy to look back and to believe that all that day I had had a sense of foreboding about my journey to come, that some sixth sense, some telepathic intuition that may lie dormant and submerged in most men, had stirred and become alert within me. But I was, in those days of my youth, a sturdy, commonsensical fellow, and I felt no uneasiness or apprehension whatsoever. Any depression of my usual blithe spirits was solely on account of the fog, and of November, and that same dreariness was shared by every citizen of London.

So far as I can faithfully recall, however, I felt nothing other than curiosity, a professional interest in what scant account of the business Mr Bentley had put before me, coupled with a mild sense of adventure, for I had never before visited that remote part of England to which I was now travelling — and a certain relief at the prospect of getting away from the unhealthy atmosphere of fog and dankness. Moreover, I was barely twenty-three years old, and retained a schoolboy's passion for everything to do with railway stations and journeys on steam locomotives.

But what is perhaps remarkable is how well I can remember the minutest detail of that day, for all that nothing untoward had yet happened, and my nerves were steady. If I close my eyes, I am sitting in the cab, crawling through the fog on my way to King's Cross Station, I can smell the cold, damp leather of the upholstery and the indescribable stench of the fog seeping in around the window, I can feel the sensation in my ears, as though they had been stuffed with cotton.

Pools of sulphurous yellow light, as from random corners of some circle of the Inferno, flared from shops and the upper windows of houses, and from the basements they rose like flares from the pit below, and there were red-hot pools of light from the chestnut-sellers on street corners; here, a great, boiling cauldron of tar for the road-menders spurted and smoked an evil red smoke, there, a lantern held high by the lamplighter bobbed and flickered.

In the streets, there was a din, of brakes grinding and horns blowing, and the shouts of a hundred drivers, slowed down and blinded by the fog, and, as I peered from out of the cab window into the gloom, what figures I could make out, fumbling their way through the murk, were like ghost figures, their mouths and lower faces muffled in scarves and veils and handkerchiefs, but on gaining the temporary safety of some pool of light they became red-eyed and demonic.

It took almost fifty minutes to travel the mile or so from chambers to the station, and as there was nothing whatsoever I could do, and I had made allowance for such a slow start to the journey, I sat back, comforting myself that this would certainly be the worst part of it, and turned over in my mind the conversation I had had with Mr Bentley that morning.

I had been working steadily at some dull details of the conveyance of property leases, forgetful, for the moment, of the fog that pressed against the window, like a furred beast at my back, when the clerk, Tomes, came in, to summon me to Mr Bentley's room. Tomes was a small man, thin as a stick and with the complexion of a tallow candle, and a permanent cold, which caused him to sniff every twenty seconds, for which reason he was confined to a cubbyhole in an outer lobby, where he kept ledgers and received visitors, with an air of suffering and melancholy that put them in mind of last wills and testaments — whatever the business they had actually come to the lawyer about.

And it was a last will and testament that Mr Bentley had before him when I walked into his large, comfortable room with its wide bay window that, on better days, commanded a fine view of the Inn of Court and gardens, and the comings and goings of half the lawyers of London. 'Sit ye down, Arthur, sit ye down.' Mr Bentley then took off his spectacles, polished them vigorously, and replaced them on his nose, before settling back in his chair, like a man content. Mr Bentley had a story to tell and Mr Bentley enjoyed being listened to.

'I don't think I ever told you about the extraordinary Mrs Drablow?'

I shook my head. It would, at any rate, be more interesting than the conveyance of leases.

'Mrs Drablow,' he repeated, and picked up the will, to wave it at me, across his partner's desk.

'Mrs Alice Drablow, of Eel Marsh House. Dead, don't you know.'

'Ah.'

'Yes. I inherited Alice Drablow, from my father. The family has had their business with this firm for . . . oh. . .' he waved a hand, back into the mists of the previous century and the foundation of Bentley, Haigh, Sweetman and Bentley.

'Oh yes?'

'A good age,' he flapped the paper again. 'Eighty-seven.'

'And it's her will you have there, I take it?'

'Mrs Drablow,' he raised his voice a little, ignoring my question which had broken into the pattern of his storytelling. 'Mrs Drablow was, as they say, a rum 'un.'

I nodded. As I had learned in my five years with the firm, a good many of Mr Bentley's older clients were 'rum 'uns.'

'Have you ever heard of the Nine Lives Causeway?'

'No, never.'

'Nor ever of Eel Marsh, in —shire?'

'No, sir.'

'Nor, I suppose, ever visited that county at all?'

'I'm afraid not.'

'Living there,' said Mr Bentley thoughtfully, 'anyone might become rum.'

'I've only a hazy idea of where it is.'

'Then, my boy, go home and pack your bags, and take the afternoon train from King's Cross, changing at Crewe and again at Homerby. From Homerby, you take the branch line to the little market town of Crythin Gifford. After that, it's a wait for the tide!'

'The *tide?*'

'You can only cross the causeway at low tide. That takes you onto Eel Marsh and the house.'

'Mrs Drablow's?'

'When the tide comes in, you're cut off until it's low again. Remarkable place.' He got up and went to the window.

'Years since I went there, of course. My father took me. She didn't greatly care for visitors.'

'Was she a widow?'

'Since quite early in her marriage.'

'Children?'

'Children.' Mr Bentley fell silent for a few moments, and rubbed at the pane with his finger, as though to clear away the obscurity, but the fog loomed, yellow-grey, and thicker than ever, though, here and there across the inn yard, the lights from other chambers shone fuzzily. A church bell began to toll. Mr Bentley turned.

'According to everything we've been told about Mrs Drablow,' he said carefully, 'no, there were no children.'

'Did she have a great deal of money or land? Were her affairs at all complicated?'

'Not on the whole, Arthur, not on the whole. She owned her house, of course, and a few properties in Crythin Gifford — shops, with tenants, that sort of thing, and there's a poor sort of farm, half under water. She spent money on a few dykes here and there, but not to much purpose. And there are the usual small trusts and investments.'

'Then it all sounds perfectly straightforward.'

'It does, does it not?'

'May I ask why I'm to go there?'

'To represent this firm at our client's funeral.'

'Oh yes, of course.'

'I wondered whether to go up myself, naturally. But, to tell you the truth, I've been troubled again by my foot this past week.' Mr Bentley suffered from gout, to which he would never refer by name, though his suffering need not have given him any cause for shame, for he was an abstemious man.

'And, then, there's the chance that Lord Boltrope will need to see me. I ought to be here, do you see?'

'Ah yes, of course.'

'And then again' — a pause — 'it's high time I put a little more onto your shoulders. It's no more than you're capable of, is it?'

'I certainly hope not. I'll be very glad to go up to Mrs Drablow's funeral, naturally.'

'There's a bit more to it than that.'

'The will?'

'There's a bit of business to attend to, in connection with the estate, yes. I'll let you have the details to read on your journey. But, principally, you're to go through Mrs Drablow's documents — her private papers — whatever they may be. *Wherever* they may be. . .' Mr Bentley grunted. 'And to bring them back to this office.'

'I see.'

'Mrs Drablow was — somewhat — disorganised, shall I say? It may well take you a while.'

'A day or two?'

'At least a day or two, Arthur. Of course, things may have changed, I may be quite mistaken . . . things may be in apple pie order and you'll clear it all up in an afternoon. As I told you, it's very many years since I went there.'

The business was beginning to sound like something from a Victorian novel, with a reclusive old woman having hidden a lot of ancient documents somewhere in the depths of her cluttered house. I was scarcely taking Mr Bentley seriously.

'Will there be anyone to help me?'

'The bulk of the estate goes to a great-niece and nephew — they are both in India, where they have lived for upwards of forty years. There used to be a housekeeper . . . but you'll find out more when you get there.'

'But presumably she had friends . . . or even neighbours?'

'Eel Marsh House is far from any neighbour.'

'And, being a rum 'un, she never made friends, I suppose?'

Mr Bentley chuckled. 'Come, Arthur, look on the bright side. Treat the whole thing as a jaunt.'

I got up.

'At least it'll take you out of all this for a day or two,' and he waved his hand towards the window. I nodded. In fact, I was not by any means unattracted to the idea of the expedition, though I saw that Mr Bentley had not been able to resist making a good story better, and dramatising the mystery of Mrs Drablow in her queer-sounding house a good way beyond the facts. I supposed that the place would merely prove cold, uncomfortable and difficult to reach, the funeral melancholy, and the papers I had to search for would be tucked under an attic bed in a dust-covered shoebox, and contain nothing more than old receipted bills and some drafts of cantankerous letters to all and sundry — all of which was usual for such a female client. As I reached the door of his room, Mr Bentley added, 'You'll reach Crythin Gifford by late this evening, and there's a small hotel you can put up at for tonight. The funeral is tomorrow morning at eleven.'

'And, afterwards, you want me to go to the house?'

'I've made arrangements . . . there's a local man dealing with it all . . . he'll be in touch with you.'

'Yes, but. . .'

Just then, Tomes materialised with a sniff at my shoulder.

'Your ten-thirty client, Mr Bentley.'

'Good, good, show him in.'

'Just a moment, Mr Bentley...'

'What is the matter, Arthur? Don't dither in the doorway, man, I've work to do.'

'Isn't there any more you ought to tell me, I...'

He waved me away impatiently, and at that point Tomes returned, closely followed by Mr Bentley's ten-thirty client. I retreated.

I had to clear my desk, go back to my rooms and pack a bag, inform my landlady that I would be away for a couple of nights, and to scribble a note to my fiancée, Stella. I rather hoped that her disappointment at my sudden absence from her would be tempered by pride that Mr Bentley was entrusting me with the firm's business in such a manner — a good omen for my future prospects upon which our marriage, planned for the following year, depended.

After that, I was to catch the afternoon train to a remote corner of England, of which until a few minutes ago I had barely heard. On my way out of the building, the lugubrious Tomes knocked on the glass of his cubbyhole, and handed me a thick brown envelope marked DRABLOW. Clutching it under my arm, I plunged out, into the choking London fog.

THE JOURNEY NORTH

As Mr Bentley had said, however far the distance and gloomy the reason for my journey, it did represent an escape from the London particular and nothing was more calculated to raise my spirits in anticipation of a treat to come than the sight of that great cavern of a railway station, glowing like the interior of a blacksmith's forge. Here, all was clangour and the cheerfulness of preparations for departure, and I purchased papers and journals at the bookstall and walked down the platform beside the smoking, puffing train, with a light step. The engine, I remember, was the Sir Bedivere.

I found a corner seat in an empty compartment, put my coat, hat and baggage on the rack and settled down in great contentment. When we pulled out of London, the fog, although still lingering about the suburbs, began to be patchier and paler, and I all but cheered. By then, a couple of other passengers had joined me in my compartment, but, after nodding briefly, were as intent on applying themselves to newspapers and other documents as myself, and so we travelled a good many uneventful miles towards the heart of England. Beyond the windows, it was quickly dark and, when the carriage blinds were pulled down, all was as cosy and enclosed as some lamplit study.

At Crewe I changed with ease and continued on my way, noting that the track began to veer towards the east, as well as heading north, and I ate a pleasant dinner. It was only when I came to change again, onto the branch line at the small station of Homerby, that I began to be less comfortable, for here the air was a great deal colder and blowing in gusts from the east with an unpleasant rain upon its breath, and the train in which I was to travel for the last hour of my journey was one of those with ancient, comfortless carriages upholstered in the stiffest of leathercloth over unyielding horsehair, and with slatted wooden racks above. It smelled of cold, stale smuts and the windows were grimed, the floor unswept.

Until the very last second, it seemed that I was to be alone not merely in my compartment but in the entire train, but, just at the blowing of the guard's whistle, a man came through the barrier, glanced quickly along the cheerless row of empty carriages and, catching sight of me at last, and clearly preferring to have a companion, climbed in, swinging the door shut as the train began to move away. The cloud of cold, damp air that he let in with him added to the chill of the compartment, and I remarked that it was a poor night, as the stranger began to unbutton his greatcoat. He looked me up and down inquisitively, though not in any unfriendly way, and then up at my things upon the rack, before nodding agreement.

'It seems I have exchanged one kind of poor weather for another. I left London in the grip of an appalling fog, and up here it seems to be cold enough for snow.'

'It'll not snow,' he said. 'The wind'll blow itself out and take the rain off with it by morning.'

'I'm very glad to hear it.'

'But, if you think you've escaped the fogs by coming up here, you're mistaken. We get bad frets in this part of the world.'

'Frets?'

'Ay, frets. Sea frets, sea mists. They roll up in a minute from sea to land across the marshes. It's the nature of the place. One minute it's as clear as a dune day, the next. . .' he gestured to indicate the dramatic suddenness of his frets. 'Terrible. But if you're staying in Crythin you won't see the worst of it.'

'I stay there tonight, at the Gifford Arms. And tomorrow morning. I expect to go out to see something of the marshes later.'

And then, not particularly wishing to discuss the nature of my business with him, I picked up my newspaper again and unfolded it with a certain ostentation, and so, for some little while, we rumbled on in the nasty train, in silence — save for the huffing of the engine, and the clanking of iron wheels upon iron rails, and occasional whistle, and the bursts of rain like sprays of light artillery fire, upon the windows.

I began to be weary, of journeying and of the cold and of sitting still while being jarred and jolted about, and to look foward to my supper, a fire and a warm bed. But in truth, and although I was hiding behind its pages, I had read my newspaper fully, and I began to speculate about my companion. He was a big man, with a beefy face and huge, raw-looking hands, well-enough spoken but with an odd accent that I took to be the local one. I put him down as a farmer, or else the proprietor of some small business. He was nearer to sixty than fifty, and his clothes were of good quality, but somewhat brashly cut, and he wore a heavy, prominent seal ring on his left hand, and that, too, had a newness and a touch of vulgarity about it. I decided that he was a man who had made, or come into, money late and unexpectedly, and was happy for the world to know it.

Having, in my youthful and priggish way, summed up and all but dismissed him, I let my mind wander back to London and to Stella, and for the rest, was only conscious of the extreme chill and the ache in my joints, when my companion startled me, by saying, 'Mrs Drablow.' I lowered my paper, and became aware that his voice echoed so loudly through the compartment because of the fact that the train had stopped, and the only sound to be heard was the moan of the wind, and a faint hiss of steam, far ahead of us.

'Drablow,' he pointed to my brown envelope, containing the Drablow papers, which I had left lying on the seat beside me.

I nodded stiffly.

'You don't tell me you're a relative?'

'I am her solicitor.' I was rather pleased with the way it sounded.

'Ah! Bound for the funeral?'

'I am.'

'You'll be about the only one that is.' In spite of myself, I wanted to find out more about the business, and clearly my companion knew it.

'I gather she had no friends — or immediate family — that she was something of a recluse? Well, that is sometimes the way with old ladies. They turn inwards — grow eccentric. I suppose it comes from living alone.'

'I daresay that it does, Mr. . . ?'

'Kipps. Arthur Kipps.'

'Samuel Daily.'

We nodded.

'And, when you live alone in such as place as that, it comes a good deal easier.'

'Come,' I said smiling, 'you're not going to start telling me strange tales of lonely houses?'

He gave me a straight look. 'No,' he said, at last, 'I am not.'

For some reason then, I shuddered, all the more because of the openness of his gaze and the directness of his manner.

'Well,' I replied in the end, 'all I can say is that it's a sad thing when someone lives for eighty-seven years and can't count upon a few friendly faces to gather together at their funeral!'

And I rubbed my hand on the window, trying to see out into the darkness. We appeared to have stopped in the middle of open country, and to be taking the full force of the wind that came howling across it. 'How far have we to go?' I tried not to sound concerned, but was feeling an unpleasant sensation of being isolated far from any human dwelling, and trapped in this cold tomb of a railway carriage, with its pitted mirror and stained, dark-wood panelling. Mr Daily took out his watch.

'Twelve miles, we're held up for the down train at Gapemouth tunnel. The hill it runs through is the last bit of high ground for miles. You've come to the flatlands, Mr Kipps.'

'I've come to the land of curious place names, certainly. This morning, I heard of the Nine Lives Causeway, and Eel Marsh, tonight of Gapemouth tunnel.'

'It's a far-flung part of the world. We don't get many visitors.'

'I suppose because there is nothing much to see.'

'It all depends what you mean by "nothing". There's the drowned churches and the swallowed-up village,' he chuckled. 'Those are particularly fine examples of "nothing to see". And we've a good wild ruin of an abbey with a handsome graveyard — you can get to it at low tide. It's all according to what takes your fancy!'

'You are almost making me anxious to get back to that London particular!'

There was a shriek from the train whistle.

27

'Here she comes.' And the train coming away from Crythin Gifford to Homerby emerged from Gapemouth tunnel and trundled past us, a line of empty yellow-lit carriages that disappeared into the darkness, and then immediately we were under way again.

'But you'll find everything hospitable enough at Crythin, for all it's a plain little place. We tuck ourselves in with our backs to the wind, and carry on with our business. If you care to come with me, I can drop you off at the Gifford Arms — my car will be waiting for me, and it's on my way.'

He seemed keen to reassure me and to make up for his teasing exaggeration of the bleakness and strangeness of the area, and I thanked him and accepted his offer, whereupon we both settled back to our reading, for the last few miles of that tedious journey.

THE FUNERAL OF MRS DRABLOW

M<small>Y FIRST IMPRESSIONS</small> of the little market town —
indeed, it seemed scarcely larger than an overgrown village
— of Crythin Gifford were distinctly favourable. When we arrived
that night, Mr Samuel Daily's car, as shining, capacious and plush
a vehicle as I had travelled in in my life, took us swiftly the bare
mile from the tiny station into the market square, where we drew
up outside the Gifford Arms.

As I prepared to alight, he handed me his card.

'Should you need anyone. . .'

I thanked him, though stressing that it was most unlikely, as I
would have whatever practical help I might require to organise
the late Mrs Drablow's business from the local agent, and did not
intend to be in the place more than a day or two. Mr Daily gave
me a straight, steady stare, and said nothing and, so as not to appear
discourteous, I tucked the card carefully into my waistcoat pocket. Only then did he give the word to his driver, and move away.

'You'll find everything hospitable enough at Crythin,' he had
said earlier, and so it proved. As I caught sight of the piled-up fire
and the capacious armchair beside it, in the parlour of the inn, and
found another fire waiting to warm me in the prettily furnished

29

bedroom at the top of the house, my spirits rose, and I began to feel rather more like a man on holiday than one come to attend a funeral, and go through the dreary business attendant upon the death of a client. The wind had either died down or else could not be heard in the shelter of the buildings, around the market square, and the discomfort, and queer trend of the conversation of my journey, faded like a bad dream.

The landlord recommended a glass of mulled wine, which I drank sitting before the fire, listening to the murmur of voices on the other side of a heavy door leading to the public bar, and his wife made my mouth water in anticipation of the supper she proposed — homemade broth, sirloin of beef, apple and raisin tart with cream, and some Stilton cheese. While I waited, I wrote a brief, fond note to Stella, which I would post the next morning, and while I ate heartily, I mused about the type of small house we might afford to live in after our marriage, if Mr Bentley were to continue to give me so much responsibility in the firm, so that I might feel justified in asking for an increase in salary.

All in all, and with the half-bottle of claret that had accompanied my supper, I prepared to go up to bed in a warm glow of well-being and contentment.

'You'll be here for the auction, I take it then, sir.' The landlord waited by the door, to bid me goodnight.

'Auction?'

He looked surprised. 'Ah — I thought you would have come up for that — there's a big auction of several farms that lie just south of here, and it's market day tomorrow as well.'

'Where is the auction?'

'Why here, Mr Kipps, in the public bar at eleven o'clock. We generally have such auctions as there are at the Gifford Arms, but there hasn't been one so big as this for a good many years. Then there's the lunch afterwards. We expect to serve upwards of forty lunches on market day, but it'll be a few more than that tomorrow.'

'Then I'm sorry I shall have to miss it — although I hope I shall be able to have a stroll round the market.'

'No intention to pry, sir — only I made sure you'd come for the auction.'

'That's all right — quite natural that you should. But at eleven o'clock tomorrow morning, I'm afraid that I have a sombre engagement. I'm here to attend a funeral — Mrs Drablow, of Eel Marsh House. Perhaps you knew of her?'

His face flickered with . . . what? Alarm, was it? Suspicion? I could not tell, but the name had stirred some strong emotion in him, all signs of which he endeavoured to suppress at once.

'I knew of her,' he said evenly.

'I am representing her firm of solicitors. I never met her. I take it she kept rather out of the way, for the most part?'

'She could hardly do otherwise, living there,' and he turned away abruptly in the direction of the public bar. 'I'll wish you goodnight, sir. We can serve breakfast at any time in the morning, to your convenience.' And he left me alone. I half moved to call him back, for I was both curious and a little irritated by his manner, and I thought of trying to get out of him exactly what he had meant by it. But I was tired and dismissed the notion, putting his remarks down to some local tales and silliness which had grown out of all proportion, as such things will do in small, out of the way communities, which have only themselves to look to for whatever melodrama and mystery they can extract out of life. For I must confess I had the Londoner's sense of superiority in those days, the half-formed belief that countrymen, and particularly those who inhabited the remoter corners of our island, were more superstitious, more gullible, more slow-witted, unsophisticated and primitive, than we cosmopolitans. Doubtless, in such a place as this, with its eerie marshes, sudden fogs, moaning winds and lonely houses, any poor old woman might be looked at askance; once upon a time, after all, she would have been branded as a witch and local legends and tales were still abroad and some extravagant folklore still half-believed in.

It was true that neither Mr Daily nor the landlord of the inn seemed anything but sturdy men of good commonsense, just as I had to admit that neither of them had done more than fall silent and look at me hard and a little oddly, when the subject of Mrs Drablow had arisen. Nonetheless, I had been left in no doubt that there was some significance in what had been left *un*said.

On the whole, that night, with my stomach full of home-cooked food, a pleasing drowsiness induced by good wine, and the sight of the low fire and inviting, turned-back covers of the deep, soft bed, I was inclined to let myself enjoy the whole business, and to be amused by it, as adding a touch of spice and local colour to my expedition, and I fell asleep most peacefully. I can recall it still, that sensation of slipping down, down into the welcoming arms of sleep, surrounded by warmth and softness, happy and secure as a small child in the nursery, and I recall waking the next morning, too, opening my eyes to see shafts of wintry sunlight playing upon the sloping white ceiling, and the delightful feeling of ease and refreshment in mind and limbs. Perhaps I recall those sensations the more vividly because of the contrast that presented with what was to come after. Had I known that my untroubled night of good sleep was to be the last such that I was to enjoy for so many terrifying, racked and weary nights to come, perhaps I should not have jumped out of bed with such alacrity, eager to be down and have breakfast, and then to go out and begin the day.

Indeed, even now in later life, though I have been as happy and at peace in my home at Monk's Piece, and with my dear wife Esmé, as any man may hope to be, and even though I thank God every night that it is all over, all long past and will not, *cannot* come again, yet I do not believe I have ever again slept so well as I did that night in the inn at Crythin Gifford. For I see that then I was still all in a state of innocence, but that innocence, once lost, is lost forever.

The bright sunshine that filled my room when I drew back the flowered curtains was no fleeting, early-morning visitor. By contrast with the fog of London, and the wind and rain of the previous evening's journey up here, the weather was quite altered as Mr Daily had confidently predicted that it would be.

Although it was early November and this a cold corner of England, when I stepped out of the Gifford Arms after enjoying a remarkably good breakfast, the air was fresh, crisp and clear and the sky as blue as a blackbird's egg. The little town was built, for the most part, of stone and rather austere grey slate, and set low, the houses huddled together and looking in on themselves. I wan-

dered about, discovering the pattern of the place — a number of straight narrow streets or lanes led off at every angle from the compact market square, in which the hotel was situated and which was now filling up with pens and stalls, carts, wagons and trailers, in preparation for the market. From all sides came the cries of men to one another as they worked, hammering tempo-rary fencing, hauling up canvas awnings over stalls, wheeling bar-rows over the cobbles. It was as cheerful and purposeful a sight as I could have found to enjoy anywhere, and I walked about with a great appetite for it all. But, when I turned my back on the square and went up one of the lanes, at once all the sounds were deadened, so that all I heard were my own footsteps in front of the quiet houses. There was not the slightest rise or slope on the ground anywhere. Crythin Gifford was utterly flat but, coming suddenly to the end of one of the narrow streets, I found myself at once in open country, and saw field after field stretching away into the pale horizon. I saw then what Mr Daily had meant about the town tucking itself in with its back to the wind, for, indeed, all that could be seen of it from here were the backs of houses and shops, and of the main public buildings in the square.

There was a touch of warmth in the autumn sunshine, and what few trees I saw, all bent a little away from the prevailing wind, still had a few last russet and golden leaves clinging to the ends of their branches. But I imagined how drear and grey and bleak the place would be in the dank rain and mist, how beaten and battered at for days on end by those gales that came sweeping across the flat, open country, how completely cut off by blizzards. That morning, I had looked again at Crythin Gifford on the map. To north, south and west there was rural emptiness for many miles — it was twelve to Homerby, the next place of any size, thirty to a large town, to the south, and about seven to any other village at all. To the east, there were only marshes, the estuary, and then the sea. For anything other than a day or two, it would certainly not do for me, but as I strolled back towards the market, I felt very much at home, and content, in the place, refreshed by the brightness of the day and fascinated by everything I saw.

When I reached the hotel again, I found that a note had been left for me in my absence by Mr Jerome, the agent who had dealt with such property and land business as Mrs Drablow had conducted, and who was to be my companion at the funeral. In a polite, formal hand, he suggested that he return at ten-forty, to conduct me to the church, and so, for the rest of the time until then, I sat in the front window of the parlour at the Gifford Arms, reading the daily newspapers and watching the preparations in the market place. Within the hotel, too, there was a good deal of activity which I took to be in connection with the auction sale. From the kitchen area, as doors occasionally swung open, wafted the rich smells of cooking, of roasting meat and baking bread, of pies and pastry and cakes, and from the dining room came the clatter of crockery. By ten-fifteen, the pavement outside began to be crowded with solid, prosperous-looking farmers in tweed suits, calling out greetings, shaking hands, nodding vigorously in discussion.

I was sad to be obliged to leave it all, dressed in my dark, formal suit and overcoat, with black armband and tie, and black hat in my hand, when Mr Jerome arrived — there was no mistaking him because of the similar drabness of his outfit — and we shook hands and went out onto the street. For a moment, standing there looking over the colourful, busy scene before us, I felt like a spectre at some cheerful feast, and that our appearance among the men in workaday or country clothes was that of a pair of gloomy ravens. And, indeed, that was the effect we seemed to have at once upon everyone who saw us. As we passed through the square we were the focus of uneasy glances, men drew back from us slightly and fell silent and stiff, in the middle of their conversations, so that I began to be unhappy, feeling like some pariah, and glad to get away and into one of the quiet streets that led, Mr Jerome indicated, directly to the parish church.

He was a particularly small man, only five feet two or three inches tall at most, and with an extraordinary, domed head, fringed around at the very back with gingerish hair, like some sort of rough braiding around the base of a lampshade. He might have been anywhere between thirty-five and fifty-seven years of age, with a blandness and formality of manner and a somewhat shuttered expression that revealed nothing whatsoever of his own personality, his mood or his thoughts. He was courteous, businesslike, and conversational but not intimate. He enquired about my journey, about the comfort of the Gifford Arms, about Mr Bentley, and about the London weather. He told me the name of the clergyman who would be officiating at the funeral, the number of properties — some half dozen — that Mrs Drablow had owned in the town and the immediate vicinity. And yet he told me nothing at all, nothing personal, nothing revelatory, nothing very interesting.

'I take it she is to be buried in the churchyard?' I asked.

Mr Jerome glanced at me sideways, and I noted that he had very large, and slightly protuberant and pale eyes of a colour somewhere between blue and grey, that reminded me of gulls' eggs.

'That is so, yes.'

'Is there a family grave?'

He was silent for a moment, glancing at me closely again, as if trying to discover whether there were any meaning behind the apparent straightforwardness of the question. Then he said, 'No. At least . . . not here, not in this churchyard.'

'Somewhere else?'

'It is . . . no longer in use,' he said, after some deliberation. 'The area is unsuitable.'

'I'm afraid I don't quite understand. . .'

But, at that moment, I saw that we had reached the church, which was approached through a wrought-iron gate, between two overhanging yew trees, and situated at the end of a particularly long very straight path. On either side, and away to the right, stood the gravestones, but to the left, there were some buildings which I took to be the church hall and — the one nearer to the church — the school, with a bell set high up in the wall, and, from within it, the sound of children's voices.

I was obliged to suspend my inquisitiveness about the Drablow family and their burial ground, and to assume, like Mr Jerome, a professionally mournful expression as we walked with measured steps towards the church porch. There, for some five minutes that seemed very much longer, we waited, quite alone, until the funeral car drew up at the gate, and from the interior of the church the parson materialised beside us; and, together, the three of us watched the drab procession of undertaker's men, bearing the coffin of Mrs Drablow, make its slow way towards us.

It was indeed a melancholy little service, with so few of us in the cold church, and I shivered as I thought once again how inexpressibly sad it was that the ending of a whole human life, from birth and childhood, through adult maturity to extreme old age, should here be marked by no blood relative or heart's friend, but only by two men connected by nothing more than business, one of whom had never so much as set eyes upon the woman during her life, besides those present in an even more bleakly professional capacity.

However, towards the end of it, and on hearing some slight rustle behind me, I half-turned, discreetly, and caught a glimpse of another mourner, a woman, who must have slipped into the church after we of the funeral party had taken our places and who stood several rows behind and quite alone, very erect and still, and not holding a prayer book. She was dressed in deepest black, in the style of full mourning that had rather gone out of fashion except, I imagined, in court circles on the most formal of occasions. Indeed, it had

clearly been dug out of some old trunk or wardrobe, for its black-
ness was a little rusty looking. A bonnet-type hat covered her head
and shaded her face, but, although I did not stare, even the swift
glance I took of the woman showed me enough to recognise that
she was suffering from some terrible wasting disease, for not only
was she extremely pale, even more than a contrast with the black-
ness of her garments could account for, but the skin and, it seemed,
only the thinnest layer of flesh was tautly stretched and strained across

her bones, so that it gleamed with a curious, blue-white sheen, and her eyes seemed sunken back into her head. Her hands that rested on the pew before her were in a similar state, as though she had been a victim of starvation. Though not any medical expert, I had heard of certain conditions which caused such terrible wasting, such ravages of the flesh, and knew that they were generally regarded as incurable, and it seemed poignant that a woman, who was perhaps only a short time away from her own death, should drag herself to the funeral of another. Nor did she look old. The effect of the illness made her age hard to guess, but she was quite possibly no more than thirty. Before I turned back, I vowed to speak to her and see if I could be of any assistance after the funeral was over, but just as we were making ready to move away, following the parson and the coffin out of the church, I heard the slight rustle of clothing once more and realised that the unknown woman had already slipped quickly away, and gone out to the waiting, open grave, though to stand some yards back, beside another headstone, that was overgrown with moss and upon which she leaned slightly. Her appearance, even in the limpid sunshine and comparative warmth and brightness outdoors, was so pathetically wasted, so pale and gaunt with disease, that it would not have been a kindness to gaze upon her; for there was still some faint trace on her features, some lingering hint, of a not inconsiderable former beauty, which must make her feel her present condition all the more keenly, as would the victim of smallpox, or of some dreadful disfigurement of burning.

Well, I thought, there is one who cares, after all, and who knows how keenly; and surely, such warmth and kindness, such courage and unselfish purpose, can never go unrewarded and unremarked, if there is any truth at all in the words that we have just heard spoken to us in the church.

And then I looked away from the woman and back, to where the coffin was being lowered into the ground, and I bent my head and prayed with a sudden upsurge of concern, for the soul of that lonely old woman, and for a blessing upon our drab circle.

When I looked up again, I saw a blackbird on the hollybush a few feet away and heard him open his mouth to pour out a sparkling fountain of song in the November sunlight, and then it was all over, we were moving away from the graveside, I a step behind Mr Jerome, as I intended to wait for the sick-looking woman and offer my arm to escort her. But she was nowhere to be seen.

While I had been saying my prayers and the clergyman had been speaking the final words of the committal, and perhaps not wanting to disturb us, or draw any attention to herself, she must have gone away, just as unobtrusively as she had arrived.

At the church gate, we stood for a few moments, talking politely, shaking hands, and I had a chance to look around me and to notice that, on such a clear, bright day, it was possible to see far beyond the church and the graveyard, to where the open marshes and the water of the estuary gleamed silver, and shone even brighter, at the line of the horizon, where the sky above was almost white and faintly shimmering.

Then, glancing back on the other side of the church, something else caught my eye. Lined up along the iron railings that surrounded the small asphalt yard of the school were twenty or so children, one to a gap. They presented a row of pale, solemn faces with great, round eyes, that had watched who knew how much of the mournful proceedings, and their little hands held the railings tight, and they were all of them quite silent, quite motionless. It was an oddly grave and touching sight, they looked so unlike children generally do, animated and carefree. I caught the eye of one and smiled at him gently. He did not smile back.

I saw that Mr Jerome waited for me politely in the lane, and I went quickly out after him.

'Tell me, that other woman. . .' I said as I reached his side. 'I hope she can find her own way home . . . she looked so dreadfully unwell. Who was she?'

He frowned.

'The young woman with the wasted face,' I urged, 'at the back of the church and then in the graveyard a few yards away from us.'

Mr Jerome stopped dead. He was staring at me.

'A young woman?'

'Yes, yes, with the skin stretched over her bones, I could scarcely bear to look at her . . . she was tall, she wore a bonnet-type of hat . . . I suppose to try and conceal as much as she could of her face, poor thing.'

For a few seconds, in that quiet, empty lane, in the sunshine, there was such a silence as must have fallen again now inside the church, a silence so deep that I heard the pulsation of the blood in the channels of my own ears. Mr Jerome looked frozen, pale, his throat moving as if he were unable to utter.

'Is there anything the matter?' I asked him quickly. 'You look unwell.'

At last he managed to shake his head — I almost would say, that he shook himself, as though making an extreme effort to pull himself together after suffering a momentous shock, though the colour did not return to his face and the corners of his lips seemed tinged with blue.

At last he said in a low voice, 'I did not see a young woman.'

'But, surely. . .' And I looked over my shoulder, back to the churchyard, and there she was again, I caught a glimpse of her black dress and the outline of her bonnet. So she had not left after all, only concealed herself behind one of the bushes or headstones, or else in the shadows of the church, waiting until we should have left, so that she could do what she was doing now, stand at the very edge of the grave in which the body of Mrs Drablow had just been laid to rest, looking down. I wondered again what connection she would have had with her, what odd story might lie behind her surreptitious visit, and what extremes of sad feeling she was now suffering, alone there. 'Look,' I said, and pointed, 'there she is again . . . ought we not to. . .' I stopped as Mr Jerome grabbed my wrist and held it in an agonisingly tight grip, and, looking at his face, was certain that he was about to faint, or collapse with some kind of seizure. I began looking wildly about me, in the deserted lane, wondering whatever I might do, where I could go, or call out, for help. The undertakers had left. Behind me were only a school of little children, and a mortally sick young woman under great emotional and physical strain, beside me was a man in a state of near-collapse. The only person I could conceivably reach was the clergyman, somewhere in the recesses of his church, and, if I were to go for him, I would have to leave Mr Jerome alone.

'Mr Jerome, can you take my arm . . . I would be obliged if you would loosen your grip a little . . . if you can just walk a few steps, back to the church . . . path . . . I saw a bench there, a little way inside the gate, you can rest and recover while I go for help . . . a car. . .'

'No!' He almost shrieked.

'But, my dear man!'

'No. I apologise. . .' He began to take deep breaths and a little colour returned by degrees to his face. 'I am so sorry. It was nothing . . . a passing faintness. . . . It will be best if you would just walk back with me towards my offices in Penn Street, off the square.'

He seemed agitated now, anxious to get away from the church and its environs.

'If you are sure. . .'

'Quite sure. Come. . .' and he began to walk quickly ahead of me, so quickly that I was taken by surprise and had to run a few steps to catch up with him. It took only a few minutes at that pace to arrive back in the square, where the market was in full cry and we were at once plunged into the hubbub of vehicles, the shouting of voices, of auctioneers and stallholders and buyers, and all the bleating and braying, the honking and crowing and cackling and whinnying of dozens of farm animals. At the sight and sound of it all, I noticed that Mr Jerome was looking better and, when we reached the porch of the Gifford Arms, he seemed almost lively, in a burst of relief.

'I gather you are to take me over to Eel Marsh House later,' I said, after pressing him to lunch with me, and being refused.

His face closed up again. He said, 'No. I shall not go there. You can cross any time after one o'clock. Keckwick will come for you. He has always been the go-between to that place. I take it you have a key?'

I nodded.

'I shall make a start on looking out Mrs Drablow's papers and getting them in some sort of order, but I suppose I shall be obliged to go across again tomorrow, and even another day after that. Perhaps Mr Keckwick can take me early in the morning, and leave me there for the whole day? I shall have to find my way about the place.'

'You will be obliged to fit in with the tides. Keckwick will tell you.'

'On the other hand,' I said, 'if it all looks as if it may take somewhat longer than I anticipate, perhaps I might simply stay there in the house? Would anyone have any objection? It seems ridiculous to expect this man to come to and fro for me.'

'I think,' said Mr Jerome carefully, 'that you would find it more comfortable to continue staying here.'

'Well, they have certainly made me welcome and the food is first rate. Perhaps you may be right.'

'I think so.'

'So long as it causes no one any inconvenience.'

'You will find Mr Keckwick perfectly obliging.'

'Good.'

'Though not very communicative.'

I smiled. 'Oh, I'm getting very used to that.' And, after shaking hands with Mr Jerome, I went to have lunch, with four dozen or so farmers.

It was a convivial and noisy occasion, with everyone sitting at three trestle tables, which were covered in long white cloths, and shouting to one another in all directions about market matters, while half a dozen girls passed in and out bearing platters of beef and pork, tureens of soup, basins of vegetables and jugs of gravy, and mugs of ale, a dozen at a time, on wide trays. Although I did not think I knew a soul in the room, and felt somewhat out of place, especially in my funeral garb, among the tweed and corduroy, I nevertheless enjoyed myself greatly, partly, no doubt, because of the contrast between this cheerful situation and the rather unnerving events of earlier in the morning. Much of the talk might have been in a foreign language, for all I understood of the references to weights and prices, yields and breeds, but, as I ate the excellent lunch, I was happy to listen all the same, and when my neighbour to the left passed an enormous Cheshire cheese to me, indicating that I should help myself, I asked him about the auction sale which had taken place in the inn earlier. He grimaced.

'The auction went according to expectations, sir. Do I take it you had an interest in the land yourself?'

'No, no. It was merely that the landlord mentioned it to me yesterday evening. I gather it was quite an important sale.'

'It disposed of a very large acreage. Half the land on the Homerby side of Crythin and for several miles east as well. There had been four farms.'

'And this land about here is valuable?'

'Some is, sir. This was. In an area where much is useless because it is all marsh and salt flat and cannot be drained to any purpose, good farming land is valuable, every inch of it. There are several disappointed men here this morning.'

'Do I take it that you are one of them?'

'Me? No. I am content with what I have and if I were not it would make no odds, for I haven't the money to take on more. Besides, I would have more sense than to pit myself against such as him.'

'You mean the successful buyer?'

'I do.'

I followed his glance across to the other table. 'Ah! Mr Daily.' For there at the far end, I recognised my travelling companion of the previous night, holding up a tankard and surveying the room with a satisfied expression.

'You know him?'

'No. I met him, just briefly. Is he a large landowner here?'

'He is.'

'And disliked because of it?'

My neighbour shrugged his broad shoulders, but did not reply.

'Well,' I said, 'if he's buying up half the county, I suppose I may be doing business with him myself before the year is out. I am a solicitor looking after the affairs of the late Mrs Alice Drablow of Eel Marsh House. It is quite possible that her estate will come up for sale in due course.'

For a moment, my companion still said nothing, only buttered a thick slice of bread and laid his chunks of cheese along it carefully. I saw by the clock on the opposite wall that it was half-past one, and I wanted to change my clothes before the arrival of Mr Keckwick, so that I was about to make my excuses and go, when my neighbour spoke. 'I doubt,' he said, in a measured tone, 'whether even Samuel Daily would go so far.'

'I don't think I fully understand you. I haven't seen the full extent of Mrs Drablow's land yet . . . I gather there is a farm a few miles out of the town. . .'

'Hoggetts!' he said in a dismissive tone. 'Fifty acres and half of it under flood for the best part of the year. Hoggetts is nothing, and it's under tenancy for his lifetime.'

'There is also Eel Marsh House and all the land surrounding it — would that be practicable for farming?'

'No, sir.'

'Well, might not Mr Daily simply want to add a little more to his empire, for the sake of being able to say that he had got it? You imply he is that type of man.'

'Maybe he is.' He wiped his mouth on his napkin. 'But let me tell you that you won't find anybody, not even Mr Sam Daily, having to do with any of it.'

'And may I ask why?'

I spoke rather sharply, for I was growing impatient of the half-hints and dark mutterings made by grown men at the mention of Mrs Drablow and her property. I had been right, this was just the sort of place where superstition and tittle-tattle were rife, and even allowed to hold sway over commonsense. Now, I expected the otherwise stalwart countryman on my left to whisper that maybe he would and, then again, maybe he would not, and how he might tell a tale, if he chose. . . . But, instead of replying to my question at all, he turned right away from me and engaged his neighbour on the other side in a complicated discussion of crops and, infuriated by the now-familiar mystery and nonsense, I rose abruptly and left the room. Ten minutes later, changed out of my funeral suit into less formal and more comfortable clothes, I was standing on the pavement awaiting the arrival of the car, driven by a man called Keckwick.

ACROSS THE CAUSEWAY

NO CAR APPEARED. Instead, there drew up outside the Gifford Arms, a rather worn and shabby pony and trap. It was not at all out of place in the market square — I had noticed a number of such vehicles that morning and, assuming that this one belonged to some farmer or stockman, I took no notice, but continued to look around me, for a motor. Then I heard my name called.

The pony was a small, shaggy-looking creature, wearing blinkers, and the driver with a large cap pulled down low over his brow, and a long, hairy brown coat, looked not unlike it, and blended with the whole equipage. I was delighted at the sight, eager for the ride, and climbed up with alacrity. Keckwick had scarcely given me a glance, and now, merely assuming that I was seated, clucked at the pony and set off, picking his way out of the crowded market square and up the lane that led to the church. As we passed it, I tried to catch a glimpse of the grave of Mrs Drablow, but it was hidden from view behind some bushes. I remembered the ill-looking, solitary young woman, too, and Mr Jerome's reaction to my mention of her. But, within a few moments, I was too caught up in the present and my surroundings to speculate any further upon the funeral and its aftermath, for we had come out into open country, and Crythin Gifford lay quite behind us, small and self-contained as it was. Now, all around and above and way beyond there seemed to be sky, sky and only a thin strip of land. I saw this part of the world as those great landscape painters had seen Holland, or the country around Norwich. Today there were no clouds at all, but I could well imagine how magnificently the huge, brooding area of sky would look with grey, scudding rain and storm clouds lowering over the estuary, how it would be here in the floods of February time when the marshes turned to iron grey and the sky seeped down into them, and in the high winds of March, when the light rippled, shadow chasing shadow across the ploughed fields.

Today, all was bright and clear, and there was a thin sun over all, though the light was pale now, the sky having lost the bright blue of the morning, to become almost silver. As we drove briskly across the absolutely flat countryside, I saw scarcely a tree, but the hedgerows were dark and twiggy and low, and the earth that had been ploughed was at first a rich mole-brown, in straight furrows. But, gradually, soil gave way to rough grass and I began to see dykes and ditches filled with water, and then we were approaching the marshes themselves. They lay silent, still and shining under the November sky, and they seemed to stretch in every direction, as far as I could see, and to merge without a break into the waters of the estuary, and the line of the horizon.

My head reeled at the sheer and startling beauty, the wide, bare openness of it. The sense of space, the vastness of the sky above and on either side made my heart race, I would have travelled a thousand miles to see this. I had never imagined such a place.

The only sounds I could hear above the trotting of the pony's hooves, the rumble of the wheels and the creak of the cart, were sudden, harsh, weird cries from birds near and far. We had travelled perhaps three miles, and passed no farm or cottage, no kind of dwelling house at all, all was emptiness. Then, the hedgerows petered out, and we seemed to be driving towards the very edge of the world. Ahead, the water gleamed like metal and I began to make out a track, rather like the line left by the wake of a boat, that ran across it. As we drew nearer, I saw that the water was lying only shallowly over the rippling sand on either side of us, and that the line was in fact a narrow track leading directly ahead, as if into the estuary itself. As we slipped onto it, I realised that this must be the Nine Lives Causeway — this and nothing more — and saw how, when the tide came in, it would quickly be quite submerged and untraceable.

As soon as the pony and then the trap met the sandy path, the smart noise we had been making ceased, and we went on almost in silence save for a hissing, silky sort of sound. Here and there were clumps of reeds, bleached bone-pale, and now and again the faintest of winds caused them to rattle dryly. The sun at our backs reflected in the water all around so that everything shone and glistened like the surface of a mirror, and the sky had taken on a faint pinkish tinge at the edges, and this in turn became reflected in the marsh and the water. Then as it was so bright that it hurt my eyes to go on staring at it, I looked up ahead, and saw, as if rising out of the water itself, a tall, gaunt house of grey stone with a slate roof, that now gleamed steelily in the light. It stood like some lighthouse or beacon or martello tower, facing the whole, wide expanse of marsh and estuary, the most astonishingly situated house I had ever seen or could ever conceivably have imagined, isolated, uncompromising but also, I thought, handsome. As we neared it, I saw the land on which it stood was raised up a little, surrounding it on every side for perhaps three or four hundred yards, of plain, salt-bleached grass, and then gravel. This little island extended in a southerly direction across an area of scrub and field towards what looked like the fragmentary ruins of some old church or chapel.

There was a rough scraping, as the cart came onto the stones, and then pulled up. We had arrived at Eel Marsh House.

For a moment or two, I simply sat looking about me in amaze-

ment, hearing nothing save the faint keening of the winter wind that came across the marsh, and the sudden rawk-rawk of a hidden bird. I felt a strange sensation, an excitement mingled with alarm . . . I could not altogether tell what. Certainly, I felt loneliness, for in spite of the speechless Keckwick and the shaggy brown pony I felt quite alone, outside that gaunt, empty house. But I was not afraid — of what could I be afraid in this rare and beautiful spot? The wind? The marsh birds crying? Reeds and still water?

I got down from the trap and walked around to the man.

'How long will the causeway remain passable?'

'Till five.'

So I should scarcely be able to do more than look around, get my bearings in the house, and make a start on the search for the

papers, before it would be time for him to return to fetch me back again. I did not want to leave here so soon, I was fascinated by it, I wanted Keckwick to be gone, so that I could wander about freely and slowly, take it all in through every one of my senses, and by myself. 'Listen,' I said, making a sudden decision, 'it will be quite ridiculous for you to be driving to and fro twice a day. The best thing will be for me to bring my bags and some food and drink and stay a couple of nights here. That way I shall finish the business a good deal more efficiently and you will not be troubled. I'll return with you later this afternoon and then, tomorrow, perhaps you could bring me back as early as is possible, according to the tides?'

I waited. I wondered if he was going to deter me, or argue, to try and put me off the enterprise, with those old dark hints. He thought for some time. But he must have recognised the firmness of my resolve at last, for he just nodded.

'Or perhaps you'd prefer to wait here for me now? Though I shall be a couple of hours. You know what suits you best.'

For answer, he simply pulled on the pony's rein, and began to turn the trap about. Minutes later, they were receding across the causeway, smaller and smaller figures in the immensity and wideness of marsh and sky, and I had turned away and walked around to the front of Eel Marsh House, my left hand touching the shaft of the key that was in my pocket.

But I did not go inside. I did not want to, yet a while. I wanted to drink in all the silence and the mysterious, shimmering beauty, to smell the strange, salt smell that was borne faintly on the wind, to listen for the slightest murmur. I was aware of a heightening of every one of my senses, and conscious that this extraordinary place was imprinting itself on my mind and deep in my imagination, too.

I thought it most likely that, if I were to stay here for any length of time, I should become quite addicted to the solitude and the quietness, and that I should turn bird-watcher, too, for there must be many rare birds, waders and divers, wild ducks and geese, especially in spring and autumn, and with the aid of books and good binoculars I should soon come to identify them by their flight and call. Indeed, as I wandered around the outside of the house, I began to speculate about living here, and to romanticise a little about how it would be for Stella and me, alone in this wild and remote spot — though the question of what I might actually do to earn our keep, and how we might occupy ourselves from day to day, I conveniently set aside.

Then, thinking thus fancifully, I walked away from the house in the direction of the field, and across it, towards the ruin. Away to the west, on my right hand, the sun was already beginning to slip down in a great, wintry, golden-red ball which shot arrows of fire and blood-red streaks across the water. To the east, sea and sky had darkened slightly to a uniform, leaden grey. The wind that came suddenly snaking off the estuary was cold.

As I neared the ruins, I could see clearly that they were indeed of some ancient chapel, perhaps monastic in origin, and all broken-down and crumbling, with some of the stones and rubble fallen, probably in recent gales, and lying about in the grass. The ground sloped a little down to the estuary shore and, as I passed under one of the old arches, I startled a bird, which rose up and away over my head with loudly beating wings and a harsh croaking cry that echoed all around the old walls and was taken up by another, some distance away. It was an ugly, satanic-looking thing, like some species of sea-vulture — if such a thing existed — and I could not suppress a shudder as its shadow passed over me, and, with relief, I watched its ungainly flight away towards the sea. Then I saw that the ground at my feet and the fallen stones between were a foul mess of droppings, and guessed that these birds must nest and roost in the walls above.

Otherwise, I rather liked this lonely spot, and thought how it would be on a warm evening at midsummer, when the breezes blew balmily from off the sea, across the tall grasses, and wild flowers of white and yellow and pink climbed and bloomed among the broken stones, the shadows lengthened gently, and June birds poured out their finest songs, with the faint lap and wash of water in the distance.

So musing, I emerged into a small burial ground. It was enclosed by the remains of a wall, and I stopped in astonishment at the sight. There were perhaps fifty old gravestones, most of them leaning over or completely fallen, covered in patches of greenish-yellow lichen and moss, scoured pale by the salt wind, and stained by years of driven rain. The mounds were grassy, and weed-covered, or else they had disappeared altogether, sunken and slipped down. No names or dates were now decipherable, and the whole place had a decayed and abandoned air.

Ahead, where the wall ended in a heap of dust and rubble, lay the grey water of the estuary. As I stood, wondering, the last light went from the sun, and the wind rose in a gust, and rustled through the grass. Above my head, that unpleasant, snake-necked bird came gliding back towards the ruins, and I saw that its beak was hooked around a fish that writhed and struggled helplessly. I watched the creature alight and, as it did so, it disturbed some of the stones, which toppled and fell out of sight somewhere.

Suddenly conscious of the cold and the extreme bleakness and eeriness of the spot and of the gathering dusk of the November afternoon, and not wanting my spirits to become so depressed that I might begin to be affected by all sorts of morbid fancies, I was about to leave, and walk briskly back to the house, where I intended to switch on a good many lights and even light a small fire if it were possible, before beginning my preliminary work on Mrs Drablow's papers. But, as I turned away, I glanced once again round the burial ground and then I saw again the woman with the wasted face, who had been at Mrs Drablow's funeral. She was at the far end of the plot, close to one of the few upright headstones, and she wore the same black clothing and bonnet, but it seemed to have slipped back so that I could make out her face a little more clearly.

In the greyness of the fading light, it had the sheen and pallor not of flesh so much as of bone itself. Earlier, when I had looked at her, although admittedly it had been scarcely more than a swift glance each time, I had not noticed any particular expression on her ravaged face, but then I had, after all, been entirely taken with the look of extreme illness. Now, however, as I stared at her, stared until my eyes ached in their sockets, stared in surprise and bewilderment at her presence, now I saw that her face did wear an expression. It was one of what I can only describe — and the words seem hopelessly inadequate to express what I saw — as a desperate, yearning malevolence; it was as though she were searching for something she wanted, needed — *must have*, more than life itself, and which had been taken from her. And, towards whoever had taken it she directed the purest evil and hatred and loathing, with all the force that was available to her. Her face, in its extreme pallor, her eyes, sunken but unnaturally bright, were burning with the concentration of passionate emotion which was within her and which streamed from her. Whether or not this hatred and malevolence was directed towards me I had no means of telling — I had no reason at all to suppose that it could possibly have been, but at that moment I was far from able to base my

reactions upon reason and logic. For the combination of the peculiar, isolated place and the sudden appearance of the woman and the dreadfulness of her expression began to fill me with fear. Indeed, I had never in my life been so possessed by it, never known my knees to tremble and my flesh to creep, and then to turn cold as stone, never known my heart to give a great lurch, as if it would almost leap up into my dry mouth and then begin pounding in my chest like a hammer on an anvil, never known myself gripped and held fast by such dread and horror and apprehension of evil. It was as though I had become paralysed. I could not bear to stay there, for fear, but nor had I any strength left in my body to turn and run away, and I was as certain as I had ever been of anything that, at any second, I would drop dead on that wretched patch of ground.

It was the woman who moved. She slipped behind the gravestone and, keeping close to the shadow of the wall, went through one of the broken gaps and out of sight.

The very second that she had gone, my nerve and the power of speech and movement, my very sense of life itself, came flooding back through me, my head cleared and, all at once, I was angry, yes, *angry*, with her for the emotion she had aroused in me, for causing me to experience such fear, and the anger led at once to determination, to follow her and stop her, and then to ask some questions and receive proper replies, to get to the bottom of it all.

I ran quickly and lightly over the short stretch of rough grass between the graves towards the gap in the wall, and came out almost on the edge of the estuary. At my feet, the grass gave way within a yard or two to sand then shallow water. All around me, the marshes and the flat salt dunes stretched away until they merged with the rising tide. I could see for miles. There was no sign at all of the woman in black, nor any place in which she could have concealed herself.

Who she was — or *what* — and how she had vanished, such questions I did not ask myself. I tried not to think about the matter at all but, with the very last of the energy that I could already feel draining out of me rapidly, I turned and began to run, to flee from the graveyard and the ruins and to put the woman at as great a distance behind as I possibly could. I concentrated everything upon my running, hearing only the thud of my own body on the grass, the escape of my own breath. And I did not look back.

By the time I reached the house again I was in a lather of sweat, from exertion and from the extremes of my emotions, and as I fumbled with the key my hand shook, so that I dropped it twice upon the step before managing at last to open the front door. Once inside, I slammed it shut behind me. The noise of it boomed through the house but, when the last reverberation had faded away, the place seemed to settle back into itself again and there was a great, seething silence. For a long time, I did not move from the dark, wood-panelled hall. I wanted company, and I had none; I needed lights and warmth and a strong drink inside me, I needed reassurance. But, more than anything else, I needed an *explanation*. It is remarkable how powerful a force simple curiosity can be. I had never realised that before now. In spite of my intense fear and sense of shock, I was consumed with the desire to find out exactly who it was that I had seen, and how. I could not rest until I had settled the business, for all that, while out there, I had not dared to stay and make any investigations.

I did not believe in ghosts. Or rather, until this day, I had not done so, and whatever stories I had heard of them I had, like most rational, sensible young men, dismissed as nothing more than stories indeed. That certain people claimed to have a stronger than normal intuition of such things and that certain old places were said to be haunted, of course I was aware, but I would have been loath to admit that there could possibly be anything in it, even if presented with any evidence. And I had never had any evidence. It was remarkable, I had always thought, that ghostly apparitions and similar strange occurrences always seemed to be experienced at several removes, by someone who had known someone who had heard of it from someone they knew!

But out on the marshes just now, in the peculiar, fading light and desolation of that burial ground, I had seen a woman whose form was quite substantial and yet in some essential respect also, I had no doubt, ghostly. She had a ghostly pallor and a dreadful expression, she wore clothes that were out of keeping with the styles of the present-day; she had kept her distance from me and she had not spoken. Something emanating from her still, silent presence, in each case by a grave, had communicated itself to me so strongly that I had felt indescribable repulsion and fear. And she had appeared and then vanished in a way that surely no real, living, fleshly human being could possibly manage to do. And yet . . . she had not looked in any way — as I imagined the traditional 'ghost' was supposed to do — transparent or vaporous, she had been real, she had been there, I had seen her quite clearly, I was certain that I could have gone up to her, addressed her, touched her.

I did not believe in ghosts.

What other explanation was there?

From somewhere in the dark recesses of the house, a clock began to strike, and it brought me out of my reverie. Shaking myself, I deliberately turned my mind from the matter of the woman in the graveyard, to the house in which I was now standing.

Off the hall ahead led a wide oak staircase and, on one side, a passage to what I took to be the kitchen and scullery. There were various other doors, all of them closed. I switched on the light in the hall but the bulb was very weak, and I thought it best to go through each of the rooms in turn and let in what daylight was left, before beginning any search for papers.

After what I had heard from Mr Bentley and from other people once I had arrived, about the late Mrs Drablow, I had had all sorts of wild imaginings about the state of her house. I had expected it, perhaps, to be a shrine to the memory of a past time, or to her youth, or to the memory of her husband of so short a time, like the house of poor Miss Haversham. Or else to be simply cobwebbed and filthy, with old newspapers, rags and rubbish piled in corners, all the debris of a recluse — together with some half-starved cat or dog.

But, as I began to wander in and out of morning room and drawing room, sitting room and dining room and study, I found nothing so dramatic or unpleasant, though it is true that there was that faintly damp, musty, sweet-sour smell everywhere about, that will arise in any house that has been shut up for some time, and particularly in one which, surrounded as this was on all sides by marsh and estuary, was bound to be permanently damp.

The furniture was old-fashioned but good, solid, dark, and it had been reasonably well looked after, though many of the rooms had clearly not been much used or perhaps even entered for years. Only a small parlour, at the far end of a narrow corridor off the hall, seemed to have been much lived in — probably it had been here that Mrs Drablow had passed most of her days. In every room were glass-fronted cases full of books and, besides the books, there were heavy pictures, dull portraits and oil paintings of old houses.

But my heart sank when, after sorting through the bunch of keys Mr Bentley had given me, I found those which unlocked various desks, bureaux, and writing tables, for in all of them were bundles and boxes of papers — letters, receipts, legal documents, notebooks, tied with ribbon or string, and yellow with age. It looked as if Mrs Drablow had never thrown away a single piece of paper or letter in her life, and, clearly, the task of sorting through these, even in a preliminary way, was far greater than I had anticipated. Most of it might turn out to be quite worthless and redundant, but all of it would have to be examined nevertheless, before anything that Mr Bentley would have to deal with, pertaining to the disposal of the estate, could be packed up and sent to London. It was obvious that there would be little point in my making a start now, it was too late and I was too unnerved by the business in the graveyard.

Instead, I simply went about the house looking in every room and finding nothing of much interest or elegance. Indeed, it was all curiously impersonal, the furniture, the decoration, the ornaments, assembled by someone with little individuality or taste, a dull, rather gloomy and rather unwelcoming home. It was remarkable and extraordinary in only one respect — its situation. From every window — and they were tall and wide in each room — there was a view of one aspect or other of the marshes and the estuary and the immensity of sky, all colour had been drained and blotted out of them now, the sun had set, the light was poor, there was no movement at all, no undulation of the water, and I could scarcely make out any break between land and water and sky. All was grey. I managed to let up every blind and to open one or two of the windows. The wind had dropped altogether, there was no sound save the faintest, softest suck of water as the tide crept in.

How one old woman had endured day after day, night after night, of isolation in this house, let alone for so many years, I could not conceive. I should have gone mad — indeed, I intended to work every possible minute without a pause to get through the papers and be done. And yet, there was a strange fascination in looking out over the wild wide marshes, for they had an uncanny beauty, even now, in the grey twilight. There was nothing whatsoever to see for mile after mile and yet I could not take my eyes away. But for today I had had enough. Enough of solitude and no sound save the water and the moaning wind and the melancholy calls of the birds, enough of monotonous greyness, enough of this gloomy old house. And, as it would be at least another hour before Keckwick would return in the pony trap, I decided that I would stir myself and put the place behind me. A good brisk walk would shake me up and put me in good heart, and work up my appetite, and if I stepped out well I would arrive back in Crythin Gifford in

The Sound of a Pony and Trap

OUTSIDE, ALL WAS QUIET, so that all I heard was the sound of my own footsteps as I began to walk briskly across the gravel, and even this sound was softened the moment I struck out over the grass towards the causeway path. Across the sky, a few last gulls went flying home. Once or twice, I glanced over my shoulder, half expecting to catch sight of the black figure of the woman following me. But I had almost persuaded myself now that there must have been some slope or dip in the ground upon the other side of that graveyard and beyond it, perhaps a lonely dwelling, tucked down out of sight, for the changes of light in such a place can play all manner of tricks and, after all, I had not actually gone out there to search for her hiding place, I had only glanced around and seen nothing. Well, then. For the time being I allowed myself to remain forgetful of the extreme reaction of Mr Jerome to my mentioning the woman that morning.

On the causeway path it was still quite dry underfoot but to my left I saw that the water had begun to seep nearer, quite silent, quite slow. I wondered how deeply the path went under water when the tide was at height. But, on a still night such as this, there was plenty of time to cross in safety, though the distance was greater, now I was traversing it on foot, than it had seemed when we trotted over in Keckwick's pony cart, and the end of the causeway path seemed to be receding into the greyness ahead. I had never been quite so alone, nor felt quite so small and insignificant in a vast landscape before, and I fell into a not unpleasant brooding, philosophical frame of mind, struck by the absolute indifference of water and sky to my presence.

Some minutes later, I could not tell how many, I came out of my reverie, to realise that I could no longer see very far in front of me and when I turned around I was startled to find that Eel Marsh House, too, was invisible, not because the darkness of evening had fallen, but because of a thick, damp sea mist that had come rolling over the marshes and enveloped everything, myself, the house behind me, the end of the causeway path and the countryside ahead. It was a mist like a damp, clinging, cobwebby thing, fine and yet impenetrable. It smelled and tasted quite different from the yellow filthy fog of London; that was choking and thick and still, this was salty, light and pale and moving in front of my eyes all the time. I felt confused, teased by it, as though it were made up of millions of live fingers that crept over me, hung on to me and then shifted away again. My hair and face and the sleeves of my coat were already damp with a veil of moisture. Above all, it was the suddenness of it that had so unnerved and disorientated me.

For a short time, I walked slowly on, determined to stick to my path until I came out onto the safety of the country road. But it began to dawn upon me that I should as likely as not become very quickly lost once I had left the straightness of the causeway, and might wander all night in exhaustion. The most obvious and sensible course was to turn and retrace my steps the few hundred yards I had come and to wait at the house until either the mist cleared, or Keckwick arrived to fetch me, or both.

That walk back was a nightmare. I was obliged to go step by slow step, for fear of veering off onto the marsh, and then into the rising water. If I looked up or around me, I was at once baffled by the moving, shifting mist, and so on I stumbled, praying to reach the house, which was farther away than I had imagined. Then, somewhere away in the swirling mist and dark, I heard the sound that lifted my heart, the distant but unmistakable clip-clop of the pony's hooves and the rumble and creak of the trap. So Keckwick was unperturbed by the mist, quite used to travelling through the lanes and across the causeway in darkness, and I stopped and waited to see a lantern — for surely he must carry one — and half wondered whether to shout and make my presence known, in case he came suddenly upon me and ran me down into the ditch.

Then I realised that the mist played tricks with sound as well as sight, for not only did the noise of the trap stay further away from me for longer than I might have expected but also it seemed to come not from directly behind me, straight down the causeway path, but instead to be away to my right, out on the marsh. I tried to work out the direction of the wind but there was none. I turned around but then the sound began to recede further away again. Baffled, I stood and waited, straining to listen through the mist. What I heard next chilled and horrified me, even though I could neither understand nor account for it. The noise of the pony trap grew fainter and then stopped abruptly and away on the marsh was a curious draining, sucking, churning sound, which went on, together with the shrill neighing and whinnying of a horse in panic, and then I heard another cry, a shout, a terrified sobbing — it was hard to decipher — but with horror I realised that it came from a child, a young child. I stood absolutely helpless in the mist that clouded me and everything from my sight, almost weeping in an agony of fear and frustration, and I knew that I was hearing, beyond any doubt, the appalling last noises of a pony and trap, carrying a child in it, as well as whatever adult — presumably Keckwick — was driving and was even now struggling desperately. It had somehow lost the causeway path and fallen into the marsh and was being dragged under by the quicksand and the pull of the incoming tide.

I began to yell until I thought my lungs would burst, and then to run forward, but then stopped, for I could see nothing and what use would that be? I could not get onto the marsh and even if I could there was no chance of my finding the pony trap or of helping its occupants; I would only, in all likelihood, risk being sucked into the marsh myself. The only thing was to get back to Eel Marsh House, to light every light and somehow try and signal with them from the windows, hoping against all reason that this would be seen, like a lightship, by someone, somewhere, in the countryside around.

Shuddering at the dreadful thoughts racing through my mind and the pictures I could not help but see of those poor creatures being slowly choked and drowned to death in mud and water, I forgot my own fears and nervous imaginings of a few minutes earlier and concentrated on getting back to the house as quickly and safely as I could. The water was now lapping very close to the edges of the path though I could only hear it, the mist was still so thick and darkness had completely fallen and it was with a gasp of relief that I felt first the turf and then the gravel beneath my feet and fumbled my way blindly to the door of the house.

Behind me, out on the marshes, all was still and silent; save for that movement of the water, the pony and trap might never have existed.

When I got inside the house again, I managed to reach a chair in that dark hall and, sitting on it just as my legs buckled beneath me, I put my head down into my hands and gave way to an outburst of helpless sobbing as the full realisation of what had just happened overcame me.

For how long I sat there, in extremes of despair and fearfulness, I do not know. But after some time I was able to pull myself together sufficiently to get up and go about the house, switching on every light that I could make work and leaving them on, though they were none of them very bright, and, in my heart, I knew that there was little chance of what was not much more than a glow from a handful of scattered lamps being seen across that misty waste land, even had there been any watcher or traveller on hand to glimpse them. But I had done something — all that I could do indeed — and I felt just fractionally better because of it. After that, I began searching in cupboards and sideboards and kitchen dressers until at last, at the very back of one such in the dining room I found a bottle of brandy — thirty years old and still fully corked and sealed. I opened it, found a glass, and poured myself as large a measure as seemed sensible to be consumed by a man in a state of great shock, some hours away from his last meal.

The room had clearly not been used by Mrs Drablow for many

years. The furniture had a faded bloom from the salt in the air and the candlesticks and épergne were tarnished, the linen cloths stiffly folded and interleaved with yellowing tissue, the glass and china dusty.

I went back into the one room in the house that had some pretensions to comfort, for all it was chilly and musty-smelling, the little sitting room, and there I sipped my brandy and tried as calmly as I could to work out what I should do.

But as the drink took effect I became more rather than less agitated and my brain was in an increasing turmoil. I began to be angry at Mr Bentley for sending me here, at my own foolish independence and block-headedness in ignoring all the hints and veiled warnings I had received about the place, and to long — no, to pray — for some kind of speedy deliverance and to be back in the safety and comforting busyness and clamour of London, among friends — indeed among any people at all — and with Stella.

I could not sit still in that claustrophobic and yet oddly hollow-feeling old house, but rambled about from room to room, lifting up this and that object and setting it down again hopelessly and then going upstairs, to wander into shuttered bedrooms and up again, to attics full of lumber, uncarpeted and without curtains or blinds at the tall narrow windows.

Every door was open, every room orderly, dusty, bitterly cold and damp and yet also somehow stifling. Only one door was locked, at the far end of a passage that led away from three bedrooms on the second floor. There was no keyhole, no bolt on the outside.

For some obscure reason, I became angry with that door, I kicked at it and rattled the handle hard, before giving up abruptly and returning downstairs, listening to the echo of my own footsteps as I went.

Every few moments, I went to one or other of the windows, rubbed my hand across the pane to try and see out; but, although I rubbed at a thin film of grime, enough to leave a clear space, I could not rub away the curtain of sea-mist that was so close up to the glass on the outside. As I stared into it I saw that it was still constantly shifting, like clouds, though without ever parting or dispersing.

At last I slumped down on the plush-covered sofa in the great, high-ceilinged drawing room, turned my face away from the window, and gave myself up, along with the last of a second glass of the mellow, fragrant brandy, to melancholy brooding and a sort of inward-looking self-pity. I was no longer cold, no longer afraid or restless, I felt cocooned against the horrible events that had taken place out on the marshes and I allowed myself to give way, to slip down into this mindless state, which was as inchoate as the fog outside, and there to rest, wallow and find, if not peace, at least a certain relief in the suspension of all extremes of emotion.

A bell was ringing, ringing, through my ears, inside my head, its clangour sounded at once very close and oddly distant, it seemed to sway, and I to sway with it, I was trying to struggle out of some darkness which was not fixed but shifting about, as the ground seemed to be shifting beneath my feet, so that I was terrified of slipping and falling down, down, of being sucked into a horrible echoing maelstrom. The bell went on ringing. I came awake in bewilderment, to see the moon, huge as a pumpkin beyond the tall windows, in a clear black sky.

My head was thick, my mouth furred and dry, my limbs stiff. I had slept, perhaps for minutes, perhaps for some hours, I had lost my sense of time. I struggled upright and then I realised that the bell I heard was not part of the confusion of my fitful nightmare but a real bell sounding through the house. Someone was at the front door.

As I half-walked, half-fell, because of numbness in my feet and legs where I had lain cramped upon the sofa, out of the room and into the hall, I began to remember what had happened and above all — and I felt an upsurge of horror as the memory returned to me — the business of the pony and trap, from which I had heard the child screaming, out upon Eel Marsh. All the lights I had left on were still shining out and must have been seen, I thought, as I pulled open the front door, hoping against hope to see a party of searchers and helpers, strong men, people to whom I could give it all over, who would know what to do and who would, above all, take me away from this place.

But in the light of the hall as it shone out and under the full moonlight too, there stood, on the gravel drive, only one man Keckwick. And behind him, the pony and trap. All seemed quite real, quite normal, and completely unharmed. The air was clear and cold, the sky thick with stars. The marshes lay still and silent and gleaming silver under the moon. There was no vestige of mist or cloud, not so much as a touch of dampness in the atmosphere. All was so changed, so utterly changed that I might have been reborn into another world and all the rest have been some fevered dream.

'You have to wait for a fret like that to clear itself. There's no crossing over while a fret's up,' Keckwick said matter-of-factly. 'Unlucky for you, that was.'

My tongue seemed to be held fast against the roof of my

mouth, my knees about to buckle beneath me.

'And, after that, there's the wait for the tide.' He looked all round him. 'Awkward place. You'll be finding that out fast enough.'

It was then that I managed to look at my watch and saw that it was almost two o'clock in the morning. The tide had just begun to recede again, revealing the Nine Lives Causeway. I had slept for almost seven hours, almost as long as I would on any normal night, but here I was with hours still to go before dawn, feeling as sick and wretched and weary as any man who has lain sleepless for hour after hour. 'I wouldn't have expected you to come back at this hour,' I managed to stammer. 'It's very good of you. . .'

Keckwick pushed his cap back a little in order to scratch at his forehead and I noticed that his nose and much of the lower part of his face were covered in bumps and lumps and warts and that the skin between was porridgy in texture and a dark, livid red. 'I wouldn't have left you over the night,' he said at last, 'wouldn't have done that to you.'

I felt a moment of light-headedness, for we seemed to have slipped into the way of normal, practical conversation — indeed, I was glad to see him, never had I welcomed the sight of a fellow human being more in my life, and to see his solid little pony that stood quietly, patiently, by.

But then the second recollection returned to me and I blurted out, 'But what happened to you, how do you manage to be here — *how did you get out?*' Then my heart lurched as I realised that of course it had not been Keckwick and his pony who had gone into the quicksand, not at all, but someone else, someone with a child, and now they were gone, dead, the marsh had taken them and the waters had closed over them and no ripple or disturbance of the faintest kind showed on that still, gleaming surface. But *who*, who, on a dark November evening in the rolling mist and the rising tide, who had been driving out, and with a child too, in that treacherous place, and why, where had they been driving to and where coming from — this was the only house for many miles, unless I had been right about the woman in black and her hidden dwelling.

Keckwick was looking straight into my face and I realised that

I must appear dishevelled and wild, not at all the businesslike, confident and smart young lawyer he had left at the house that afternoon. Then he indicated the pony trap: 'Best get in,' he said.

'Yes — but surely. . .'

He had turned away abruptly and was climbing into the driving seat. There, looking straight ahead of him, huddled into his greatcoat with the collar turned to cover his neck and chin, he waited. That he was fully aware of my state, knew something had happened to me and was quite unsurprised, was clear, and his manner also told me unmistakably that he did not wish to hear what it was, to ask or answer questions, to discuss the business at all. He would fetch and carry and that reliably and at any hour and he would do no more.

Silently, quickly, I went back into the house and switched off the lights and then I got into the cart and let Keckwick and his pony take me away, across the quiet, eerily beautiful marshes, under the riding moon. I fell into a sort of trance, half sleeping, half waking, rocked by the motion of the cart. My head had begun to ache miserably and my stomach to contract with spasms of nausea now and again. I did not look about me, though sometimes I glanced up into the great bowl of the night sky and at the constellations scattered there and the sight was comforting and calming to me, things in the heavens seemed still to be aright and unchanged. But nothing else was, within me or all around. I knew now that I had entered some hitherto unimagined — indeed, unbelieved-in — realm of consciousness, that coming to this place had already changed me and that there was no going back. For, today, I had seen things I had never dreamed of seeing and heard things too. That the woman by the graves had been ghostly I now — not believed, no — I *knew*, for certainty lay deep within me, I realised that it had become fixed and immovable, perhaps during that restless, anguished sleep. But I began to suspect that the pony and trap that I had heard out on the marsh, the pony and trap with the child who had cried out so terribly and which had been sucked into the quicksands, while marsh and estuary, land and sea, had been shrouded in that sudden fog and I lost in the midst of it — they, too, had not been real, not there, present, not substantial, but ghostly also. What I had heard, I had heard, as clearly as I now heard the roll of the cart and the drumming of the pony's hooves, and what I had seen — the woman with the pale, wasted face, by the grave of Mrs Drablow and again in the old burial ground — I had seen. I would have sworn to that on oath, on any testament. Yet they had been, in some sense I did not understand, unreal, ghostly, things that were dead.

Having accepted so much, I at once felt calmer and so we left the marsh and the estuary behind us and cropped along the lane in the middle of that quiet night. I supposed that the landlord of the Gifford Arms could be knocked up and persuaded to let me in, and then I intended to go up to that comfortable bed and sleep again, to try and shut out all these things from my head and my heart and not think of them more. Tomorrow, in daylight, I would recover myself and then plan what I was going to do. At this moment I knew that more than anything else I did not want to have to go back to Eel Marsh House and must try to find some way of extricating myself from any more dealings with the affairs of Mrs Drablow. Whether I would make some excuse to Mr Bentley or endeavour to tell him the truth and hope not to be ridiculed I did not try and decide.

It was only as I was getting myself ready for bed — the landlord having proved most sympathetic and accommodating — that I began to think again about the extraordinary generosity of Keckwick, in coming out for me the moment the mist and tides enabled him to do so. He would surely have been expected to shrug his shoulders, retire and plan to collect me first thing in the morning. But he must have waited up and perhaps even kept his pony harnessed, in his concern that I should not have to spend a night alone in that house. I was profoundly grateful to him and I made a note that he should receive a generous reward for his pains.

It was after three o'clock when I climbed into bed, and it would not be light for another five hours. The landlord had said I was to sleep on as long as I chose, no one would disturb me and a breakfast would be provided at any time. He, too, in his different way, had seemed as anxious for my welfare as Keckwick, though about them both there was the same extreme reserve, a barrier put up against all enquiry which I had the sense not to try and break down. Who could tell what they themselves had seen or heard, how much more they knew about the past and all manner of events, not to mention rumours and hearsay and superstition about those events, I could not guess. The little I had experienced was more than enough and I was reluctant to begin delving into any explanations.

So I thought that night, as I laid my head on the soft pillow and fell eventually into a restless, shadowy sleep, across which figures came and went, troubling me, so that once or twice I half-woke myself, as I cried out or spoke a few incoherent words, I sweated, I turned and turned about, trying to free myself from the nightmares, to escape from my own semiconscious sense of dread and foreboding, and all the time, piercing through the surface of my dreams, came the terrified whinnying of the pony and the crying and calling of that child over and over, while I stood, helpless in the mist, my feet held fast, my body pulled back, and while behind me, though I could not see, only sense, her dark presence hovered the woman.

Mr Jerome Is Afraid

WHEN I AWOKE, it was again to see the pleasant bedroom filled with bright winter sunshine. But it was with a great sense of weariness and bitterness, too, that I contrasted my present state with that of the previous morning, when I had slept so well and woken so refreshed and sprung out of bed eager to begin the day. And was it only yesterday? I felt as if I had journeyed so far, in spirit if not in time, experienced so much and been so churned about within my formerly placid and settled self that it might have been years since then. Now, I felt heavy and sick in my head, stale and tired and jangled too, my nerves and my imagination were all on edge.

But, after a while, I forced myself to rise, as I could hardly feel worse than I did lying in the bed that now felt as lumpish and uncomfortable as a heap of potato sacks. Once I had drawn back the curtains on a sharp blue sky and taken a good hot bath, followed by a rinse of my head and neck under the cold tap, I began to feel less frowsty and depressed, more composed and able to think in an orderly way about the day ahead. Over breakfast, for which I had a better appetite than I had expected, I put to myself the various alternatives. Last night I had been adamant and would have brooked no possible opposition — I was having nothing more to do with Eel Marsh and the Drablow business but would telegraph to Mr Bentley, leave matters in the hands of Mr Jerome and take the first available train to London.

In short, I was going to run away. Yes, that was how I saw it in the bright light of day. I attached no particular blame to my decision. I had been as badly frightened as a man could be. I did not think that I would be the first to run from physical risks and dangers, although I had no reason to suppose myself markedly braver than the next person. But these other matters were altogether more terrifying, because they were intangible and inexplicable, incapable of proof and yet so deeply affecting. I began to realise that what had frightened me most — and, as I investigated my own thoughts and feelings that morning, what continued to frighten me — was not what I had seen — there had been nothing intrinsically repellent or horrifying about the woman with the wasted face. It was true that the ghastly sounds I had heard through the fog had greatly upset me but far worse was what emanated from and surrounded these things and arose to unsteady me, an atmosphere, a force — I do not exactly know what to call it — of evil and uncleanness, of terror and suffering, of malevolence and bitter anger. I felt quite at a loss to cope with any of these things.

'You'll find Crythin a quieter place today,' the landlord said, as he came to clear away my plate and replenish my pot of coffee. 'Market day brings everyone from miles about. There'll be little enough happening this morning.'

He stood for a moment, looking at me closely, and I again felt it necessary to apologise for having had him get up and come down to let me in, the previous night. He shook his head. 'Oh, I had rather that than have you spend an ... an uncomfortable night anywhere else.'

'As it happened, my night was a bit disturbed in any case. I seemed to have an overdose of bad dreams and be generally restless.'

He said nothing.

'I think what I need this morning is some exercise in the fresh air. Perhaps I'll walk into the countryside a mile or so, look at the farms belonging to some of the men who were all here doing their market business yesterday.'

What I meant was that I planned to turn my back upon the marshes and walk steadfastly in the opposite direction.

'Well, you'll find it nice and easy walking, we're flat as a bed-sheet for many miles about. Of course, you could go a good deal further, if you want to be on horseback.'

'Alas, I have never ridden in my life and I confess I don't feel in the mood to start today.'

'Or else,' he said suddenly with a smile, 'I can lend you a good stout bicycle.'

A bicycle! He saw my expression change. As a boy I had bicycled regularly and far, and indeed Stella and I still sometimes took the train out towards one of the locks and cycled for miles along the Thames towpath with a picnic in our baskets.

'You'll find it around the back, in the yard there. Just help yourself, sir, if the fancy takes you.' And he left the dining room.

The idea of bicycling for an hour or so, to blow away the clinging cobwebs and staleness of the night, to refresh and restore me, was extremely cheering, and I knew that my mood was uprising. Moreover, I was not going to run away.

Instead, I decided to go and talk to Mr Jerome. I had formed some notion of asking for help in sorting out Mrs Drablow's papers — perhaps he had an office boy he could spare, for I was now sure that, in daylight and with company, I was strong enough again to face Eel Marsh House. I would return to the town well before dark and work as methodically and efficiently as possible. Nor would I take any walk in the direction of the burial ground.

It was remarkable how physical well-being had improved my spirits and, as I stepped outside into the market square, I felt once again my normal, equable, cheerful self, while every so often a spurt of glee arose inside me at the anticipation of my bicycle ride.

I found the office of Horatio Jerome, Land and Estate Agent — two pokey, low-ceilinged rooms, over a corn merchant's store, in the narrow lane leading off the square — and expected also to find an assistant or clerk, to whom to give my name. But there was no one. The place was silent, the outer waiting room dingy and empty. So after hovering about for a few moments I went to the only other closed door and knocked. There was a further pause and then the scraping of a chair and some quick footsteps. Mr Jerome opened the door.

It was clear at once that he was by no means pleased to see me. His face took on the closed-up, deadened look of the previous day and he hesitated before eventually inviting me into his office and cast odd, half-glances at me, before looking quickly away again, to a point over my shoulder. I paused, waiting, I suppose, for him to enquire how I had fared at Eel Marsh House. But he said nothing at all and so I began to put my proposal to him.

'You see I had had no idea — I don't know whether you had — of the volume of papers belonging to Mrs Drablow. Tons of the stuff and most of it I've no doubt so much waste, but it will have to be gone through item by item, nevertheless. It seems clear that, unless I am to take up residence in Crythin Gifford for the foreseeable future, I shall have to have some help.'

Mr Jerome's expression was one of panic. He shifted his chair back, further away from me, as he sat behind his rickety desk, so that I thought that, if he could have gone through the wall into the street, he would like to have done so.

'I'm afraid *I* can't offer you help, Mr Kipps. Oh, no.'

'I wasn't thinking that you would do anything personally,' I said in a soothing tone. 'But perhaps you have a young assistant.'

'There is no one. I am quite on my own. I cannot give you any help at all.'

'Well then, help me to find someone — surely the town will yield me a young man with a modicum of intelligence, and keen to earn a few pounds, whom I may take on for the job?'

I noticed that his hands, which rested on the sides of his chair, were working, rubbing, fidgeting, gripping and ungripping in agitation.

'I'm sorry — this is a small place — young people leave — there are no openings.'

'But I am offering an opening — albeit temporary.'

'You will find no one suitable.' He was almost shouting at me.

Then I said, very calmly and quietly, 'Mr Jerome, what you

mean is not that there is no one available, that no young person — or older person for that matter — could be found in the town or the neighbourhood able and free to do the work if a thorough search were to be made. There would not I am sure be many applicants but certainly we should be able to find one or two possible candidates for the job. But you are backing away from speaking out the truth of the matter, which is that I should not find a soul willing to spend any time out at Eel Marsh House, for fear of the stories about that place proving true — for fear of encountering what I have already encountered.'

There was absolute silence. Mr Jerome's hands continued to scrabble about like the paws of some struggling creature. His pale domed forehead was beaded with perspiration. Eventually he got up, almost knocking over his chair as he did so, and went over to the narrow window to look out through the dirty pane onto the houses opposite and down into the quiet lane below. Then, with his back to me, he said at last, 'Keckwick came back for you.'

'Yes. I was more grateful than I can say.'

'There's nothing Keckwick doesn't know about Eel Marsh House.'

'Do I take it he fetched and carried sometimes for Mrs Drablow?'

He nodded. 'She saw no one else. Not —' his voice trailed away.

'Not another living soul,' I put in evenly.

When he spoke again he sounded husky and tired. 'There are stories,' he said, 'tales. There's all that nonsense.'

'I can believe it. Such a place would breed marsh monsters and creatures of the deep and jack-o'-lanterns by the cartload.'

'You can discount most of it.'

'Of course. But not all.'

'You saw that woman in the churchyard.'

'I saw her again. I went for a walk all around the ground Eel Marsh House stands on, after Keckwick had left me yesterday afternoon. She was in that old burial ground. What are the ruins — some church or chapel?'

'There was once a monastery on that island — long before the house was ever built. Some small community that cut itself off

from the rest of the world. There are records of it in the county histories. It was abandoned, left to decay — oh, centuries ago.'

'And the burial ground?'

'There was . . . some later use. A few graves.'

'The Drablows?'

He turned suddenly to face me. There was a sickly greyish pallor over his skin now and I realised how seriously he was affected by our conversation and that he would probably prefer not to continue. I had to make my arrangements but I decided, at that moment, to abandon the attempt to work with Mr Jerome and to telephone instead, directly to Mr Bentley in London. For that purpose, I would return to the hotel.

'Well,' I said, 'I'm not going to be put out by a ghost or several ghosts, Mr Jerome. It was unpleasant and I confess that I shall be glad when I have found a companion to share my work out at the house. But it will have to be done. And I doubt if the woman in black can have any animosity towards *me*. I wonder who she was? *Is?*' I laughed though it came out sounding quite false into the room. 'I hardly know how to refer to her!'

I was trying to make light of something that we both knew was gravely serious, trying to dismiss as insignificant, and perhaps even nonexistent, something that affected us both as deeply as any other experience we had undergone in our lives, for it took us to the very edge of the horizon where life and death meet together. 'I must face it out, Mr Jerome. Such things one must face.' And even as I spoke I felt a new determination arise within me.

'So I said.' Mr Jerome was looking at me pityingly. 'So I said . . . once.'

But his fear was only serving to strengthen my resolve. He had been weakened and broken, by what? A woman? A few noises? Or was there more that I should discover for myself? I knew that, if I asked him, he would refuse to answer and, in any case, I was uncertain whether I wanted to be filled up with all these frightening and weird tales of the nervous Mr Jerome's past experiences at Eel Marsh House. I decided that, if I were to get to the truth of the business, I should have to rely upon the evidence of my own senses and nothing more. Perhaps, after all, I should do better *not* to have an assistant.

I took my leave of Mr Jerome, remarking as I went that in all probability I should see nothing more of the woman or of any other peculiar visitors to the late Mrs Drablow's house.

'I pray that you do not,' Mr Jerome said, and he held onto my hand with a sudden fierce grip as he shook it. 'I pray that you do not.'

'Don't worry about it,' I called, deliberately making myself sound carefree and cheerful, and I ran lightly down the staircase, leaving Mr Jerome to his agitation.

I returned to the Gifford Arms and, instead of telephoning, wrote a letter to Mr Bentley. In it I described the house and its hoard of papers and explained that I should have to stay longer than anticipated and that I expected to hear if Mr Bentley required me to return at once to London, and make some other arrangements. I also made a light remark about the bad reputation Eel Marsh House enjoyed locally and said that for this reason — but also for others rather more mundane — it might be difficult for me to get any help, though I was anxious to try. The whole business, nevertheless, should be completed within the week and I would arrange for the dispatch of as many papers as seemed to be important to London.

Then, putting the letter on the table in the lobby, to be collected at noon, I went out and found the landlord's bicycle, a good, old-fashioned sit-up-and-beg with a large basket on the front almost like that sported by the butcher-boys in London. I mounted it and pedalled out of the square and away, up one of the side streets towards the open country. It was the perfect day for bicycling, cold enough to make the wind burn against my cheeks as I went, bright and clear enough for me to be able to see a long way in all directions across that flat, open landscape.

I intended to cycle to the next village, where I hoped to find another country inn and enjoy some bread and cheese and beer for lunch but, as I reached the last of the houses, I could not resist the urge that was so extraordinarily strong within me to stop and look, not westwards, where I might see farms and fields and the distant roofs of a village, but east. And there they lay, those glittering, beckoning, silver marshes with the sky pale at the horizon where it reached down to the water of the estuary. A thin breeze blew off them with salt on its breath. Even from as far away as this I could hear the mysterious silence, and once again the haunting, strange beauty of it all aroused a response deep within me. I could not run away from that place, I would have to go back to it, not now, but soon. I had fallen under some sort of spell of the kind that certain places exude and it drew me, my imaginings, my longings, my curiosity, my whole spirit, towards itself.

For a long time, I looked and looked and recognised what was happening to me. My emotions had now become so volatile and so extreme, my nervous responses so near the surface, so rapid and keen, that I was living in another dimension, my heart seemed to beat faster, my step to be quicker, everything I saw was brighter, its outlines more sharply, precisely defined. And all this since yesterday. I had wondered whether I looked different in some essential way so that, when I eventually returned home, my friends and family would notice the change. I felt older and like a man who was being put to trial, half fearful, half wondering, excited, completely in thrall.

SPIDER

I RETURNED some four hours and thirty-odd miles later in a positive glow of well-being. I had ridden out determinedly across the countryside, seeing the very last traces of a golden autumn merging into the beginnings of winter, feeling the rush of pure cold air on my face, banishing every nervous fear and morbid fancy by energetic physical activity. I had found my village inn and eaten my bread and cheese and even, afterwards, made myself free of a farmer's barn to sleep for an hour.

Coming back into Crythin Gifford I felt like a new man, proud, satisfied, and most of all eager and ready to face and to tackle the worst that Mrs Drablow's house and those sinister surrounding marshes might have in store for me. In short, I was defiant, defiant and cheerful, and so I spun around a corner into the square and almost smack into a large motor car which was negotiating the narrow turn in the oncoming direction. As I swerved, braked and scrambled somehow off my machine, I saw that the car belonged to my railway travelling companion, the man who had been buying up farms at yesterday's auction, Mr Samuel Daily.

Now, he was bidding his driver slow down and leaning out of the window to ask me how I did.

'I've just had a good spin out into the countryside and I shall do justice to my dinner tonight,' I said cheerfully.

Mr Daily raised his eyebrows. 'And your business?'

'Mrs Drablow's estate? Oh, I shall soon have all that in order, though I confess there will be rather more to do than I had anticipated.'

'You have been out to the house?'

'Certainly.'

'Ah.'

For a few seconds we looked at each other, neither one apparently willing to press the subject a little further. Then, preparing to remount my bicycle once I was out of his way, I said breezily, 'To tell the truth, I'm enjoying myself. I am finding the whole thing rather a challenge.'

Mr Daily continued to regard me steadily until I was forced to shift about and glance away, feeling like nothing so much as a schoolboy caught out in blustering his way through a fabricated tale.

'Mr Kipps,' he said, 'you are whistling in the dark. Let me give you that dinner you say you've such an appetite for. Seven o'clock. Your landlord will direct you to my house.' Then he motioned to the driver, sat back and did not give me another glance.

Once back at the hotel, I began to make serious arrangements for the next day or so for, although there had been a grain of truth in Mr Daily's accusation, I was nonetheless in a firmly determined frame of mind and more than ready to go ahead with the business at Eel Marsh House. Accordingly, I asked for a hamper of provisions to be got ready and, in addition, went out myself into the town and bought some additional supplies — packets of tea and coffee and sugar, a couple of loaves of bread, a tin of biscuits, fresh pipe tobacco, matches and so forth. I also purchased a large torch lantern and a pair of wellington boots. Far at the back of my mind, I retained a vivid recollection of my walk on the marshes in the fog and rising tide. If that were ever to happen again —

though I prayed fervently it would not — I determined to be as well prepared, at least for any physical eventuality, as I could be. When I told the landlord of my plan — that I intended to spend tonight at his inn and then the next two over at Eel Marsh House he said nothing at all but I knew full well that he was recalling at the same moment as I was myself how I had arrived, banging violently on his door in the early hours of that morning, the shock from my experiences etched upon my face. When I asked if I could again borrow the bicycle he merely nodded. I told him that I wanted to retain my room and that, depending on how speedily I got through the work on Mrs Drablow's papers, I should be taking my final leave towards the end of the week.

I have often wondered since what the man actually thought of me and the enterprise I was blithely undertaking, for it was clear that he knew as much as anyone not only of the stories and rumours attaching to Eel Marsh House but of the truth too. I suspect that he would have preferred me to be gone altogether but was making it his business neither to voice an opinion nor to give warning or advice. And my manner that day must have indicated clearly that I would brook no opposition, heed no warning, even from within myself. I was by now almost pigheadedly bent upon following my course.

That much Mr Samuel Daily ascertained within a few moments of my arriving at his house that evening and he watched me and let me babble, saying nothing himself for the best part of our meal.

I had found my way there without difficulty and been duly impressed upon my arrival. He lived in an imposing, rather austere country park, which reminded me of something that a character in the novels of Jane Austen might have inhabited, with a long, tree-lined carriage drive up to a porticoed front, stone lions and urns mounted upon pillars on either side of a short flight of steps, a balustraded walk, overlooking rather dull, formal lawns with close-clipped hedges. The whole effect was grand and rather chilling and somehow quite out of keeping with Mr Daily himself. He had clearly bought the place because he had made enough money to do so and because it was the biggest house for miles around but, having bought it, he did not seem very much at ease within it and I wondered how many rooms stood empty and unused for much of the time, for apart from a few household staff only he and his wife lived here, though they had one son, he told me, married and with a child of his own.

Mrs Daily was a quiet, shy-seeming, powdery-looking little woman, even more ill at ease in her surroundings than he. She said little, smiled nervously, crocheted something elaborate with very fine cotton.

Nonetheless, they both made me warmly welcome, the meal was an excellent one, of roast pheasant and a huge treacle tart, and I began to feel comfortably at home.

Before and during supper and over coffee, which Mrs Daily poured out for us in the drawing room, I listened to the story of Samuel Daily's life and rising fortunes. He was not so much boastful, as exuberantly gleeful, at his own enterprise and good luck. He listed the acres and properties he owned, the number of men in his employ or who were his tenants, told me of his plans for the future which were, so far as I could ascertain, simply to become the biggest landlord in the county. He talked about his son and his young grandson too, for both of whom he was building up this empire. He might be envied and resented, I thought, particularly by those who competed with him for the purchase of land and property. But he could surely not be disliked, he was so simple, so direct, so unashamed of his ambitions. He seemed astute and yet unsubtle, a keen bargainer, but thoroughly honest. As the evening went on I found myself taking to him more and more warmly and confiding in him too, telling him of my own albeit small-seeming ambitions, if Mr Bentley would give me a chance, and about Stella and our prospects for the future.

It was not until the timid Mrs Daily had retired and we were in the study, a decanter of good port and another of whisky on the small table between us, that my reason for being in the area was so much as referred to.

Mr Daily poured me a generous glass of port wine and as he handed it over said, 'You're a fool if you go on with it.'

I took a sip or two calmly and without replying, though something in the bluntness and abruptness of his speaking had given rise to a spurt of fear deep within me, which I suppressed at once.

'If you mean you think I should give up the job I've been sent here to do and turn tail and run. . .'

'Listen to me, Arthur.' He had begun to use my Christian name in an avuncular way, while not offering me the use of his. 'I'm not going to fill you up with a lot of women's tales . . . you'd find those out fast enough if you ask about the places. Maybe you already have.'

'No,' I said, 'only hints — and Mr Jerome turning a little pale.'

'But you went out there to the place.'

'I went there and I had an experience I shouldn't care to go through again, though I confess I can't explain it.'

And then I told him the full story, of the woman with the wasted face at the funeral and in the old burial ground, and of my walk across the marsh in the fog and the terrible sounds I had heard there. He sat impassively, a glass at his hand and listened without interrupting me until I had reached the end.

'It seems to me, Mr Daily,' I said, 'that I have seen whatever ghost haunts Eel Marsh and that burial ground. A woman in black with a wasted face. Because I have no doubt at all that she was whatever people call a ghost, that she was not a real, living, breathing human being. Well, she did me no harm. She neither spoke nor

came near me. I did not like her look and I liked the . . . the power that seemed to emanate from her towards me even less, but I have convinced myself that it is a power that cannot do more than make me feel afraid. If I go there and see her again, I am prepared.'

'And the pony and trap?'

I could not answer because, yes, that had been worse, far worse, more terrifying because it had been only heard not seen and because the cry of that child would never, I was sure, leave me for the rest of my life.

I shook my head. 'I won't run away.'

I felt strong, sitting there at Samuel Daily's fireside, resolute, brave and stout-hearted, and I also — and he saw it — felt proud of being so. Thus, I thought, would a man go into battle, thus armed would he fight with giants.

'You shouldn't go there.'

'I'm afraid I'm going.'

'You shouldn't go there alone.'

'I could find no one to go with me.'

'No,' he said, 'and you would not.'

'Good God, man, Mrs Drablow lived alone there for — what was it? — sixty odd years — to a ripe old age. She must have come to terms with all the ghosts about the place.'

'Ay.' He stood up. 'Maybe that's just what she did do. Come — Bunce will take you home.'

'No — I'd prefer to walk. I'm getting a taste for fresh air.' As it happened, I had come on the bicycle but, confronted with the grandeur of the Daily home, had hidden it in a ditch beyond the outer gates, feeling that it did not look quite right to bicycle up that carriage drive.

As I thanked him for the evening's hospitality and was getting into my coat, he seemed to be mulling something over, and at the last moment he said suddenly, 'You are still set on it?'

'I am.'

'Then take a dog.'

I laughed. 'I haven't got a dog.'

'I have.' And he strode in front of me, out of the house, down the steps and into the darkness at the side of the house where presumably the outbuildings were situated. I waited, amused, and rather touched by his concern for me, speculating idly about what use a dog would be against any spectral presence, but not reluctant to take up Mr Daily's offer. I liked dogs well enough and it would be a fellow creature, warm-blooded and breathing in that cold, empty old house.

After a few moments there came the pat and scrabble of feet, followed by Mr Daily's measured tread.

'Take her,' he said, 'bring her back when you are done.'

'Will she come with me?'

'She'll do what I tell her.'

I looked down. At my feet stood a sturdy little terrier with a rough brindle coat and bright eyes. She wagged her tail briefly, acknowledging me, but otherwise was still, close to Daily's heels.

'What's her name?'

'Spider.'

The dog's tail flicked again.

'All right,' I said, 'I'll be glad of her company, I confess. Thank you.' I turned and began to walk off down the broad drive. After a few yards I turned and called. 'Spider. Here. Come, girl. Spider.' The dog did not stir and I felt foolish. Then Samuel Daily chuckled, snapped his fingers and spoke a word. At once, Spider bounded after me and stuck obediently to my heels.

I retrieved the bicycle, when I was sure that I could no longer be seen from the house, and the dog ran cheerfully after me down the quiet, moonlit lane, towards the town. My spirits rose. In a strange way, I was looking forward to the morrow.

In the Nursery

THE FINE CLEAR WEATHER still held, there was sunshine and blue sky again, when I drew my curtains. I had slept lightly and restlessly, troubled by snatches of peculiar, disconnected dreams. Perhaps I had eaten and drunk too well and richly with Mr Daily. But my mood was unchanged, I was determined and optimistic, as I dressed and breakfasted, and then began to make preparations for my stay at Eel Marsh House. The little dog Spider had, somewhat to my surprise, slept motionlessly at the foot of my bed. I had taken to her, though I knew little of the way of dogs. She was spirited, lively and alert and yet completely biddable, the expression in her bright eyes, fringed a little by shaggy hair that formed itself somewhat comically into the shape of beetling eyebrows, seemed to me highly intelligent. I thought I was going to be very glad of her.

Just after nine o'clock the landlord summoned me to the telephone. It was Mr Bentley, crisp and curt — for he greatly disliked using the instrument. He had received my letter and agreed that

I should stay until I had at least made some sort of sense of the Drablow papers and managed to sort out what looked as if it needed to be dealt with, from all the out-of-date rubbish. I was to parcel up and dispatch anything I thought important, leave the remainder in the house for the attention of the legatees at some future date and then return to London.

'It's an odd sort of place,' I said.

'She was an odd sort of woman.' And Mr Bentley clapped the receiver down hard, blistering my ear.

By nine-thirty I had the bicycle basket and panniers packed and ready, and I set off, Spider bounding behind me. I could not leave it any later or the tide would have risen across the causeway and it occurred to me, as I bowled over the wide open marshes, that I was burning my boats, at least in a small way — if I had left anything important behind, I could not return to fetch it for some hours.

The sun was high in the sky, the water glittering, everywhere was light, light and space and brightness, the very air seemed somehow purified and more exhilarating. Sea birds soared and swooped, silver-grey and white, and ahead, at the end of the long straight path, Eel Marsh House beckoned to me.

For half an hour or so after my arrival, I worked busily at establishing myself there, domestically. I found crockery and cutlery in the somewhat gloomy kitchen at the back of the house, washed, dried and laid it out for my later use and made over a corner of the larder to my provisions. Then, after searching through drawers and cupboards upstairs, I found clean linen and blankets and set them to air before a fire I had built in the drawing room. I made other fires too, in the little parlour and in the dining room, and even succeeded, after some trial and error, in getting the great black range alight, so that by evening I hoped to have hot water for a bath.

Then I let up the blinds and opened some windows and established myself at a large desk in one of the bays of the morning room that had, I thought, the finest view of the sky, the marshes, the estuary. Beside me, I set two chests of papers. Then, with a pot of tea at my right hand and the dog Spider at my feet, I commenced work. It was pretty tedious going but I persevered patiently enough, untying and cursorily examining bundle after bundle of worthless old papers, before tossing them into an empty box I had set beside me for the purpose. There were ancient household accounts and tradesmen's bills and receipts of thirty and forty years or more before; there were bankers' statements and doctors' prescriptions and estimates from carpenters, glaziers and decorators; there were many letters from persons unknown — and Christmas and anniversary cards, though nothing dating from recent years. There were accounts from department stores in London and scraps of shopping lists and measurements.

Only the letters themselves I reserved for later perusal. Everything else was waste. From time to time, to alleviate the boredom, I looked out of the wide windows at the marshes, unshadowed still and quietly beautiful in the winter sunlight. I made myself a lunch of ham and bread and beer and then, a little after two o'clock, I called to Spider and went outside. I felt very calm and cheerful, a little cramped after my morning spent at the desk, a little bored, but in no way nervous. Indeed, all the horrors and apparitions of my first visit to the house and the marshes had quite evaporated, along with the mists that had for that short time engulfed me. The air was crisp and fresh and I walked all around the perimeter of the land upon which Eel Marsh House stood, occasionally tossing a stick for the dog to chase happily after and retrieve, breathing in the clean air deeply, entirely relaxed. I even ventured as far as the ruin of the burial ground and Spider dashed in and out, searching for real or imaginary rabbits, digging occasionally in a frantic burst with her front paws and then bounding excitedly away. We saw no one. No shadow fell across the grass.

For a while, I wandered among the old gravestones, trying to decipher some of the names but without any success, until I reached the corner where, that last time, the woman in black had been standing. There, on the headstone against which — I was fairly certain I remembered aright — she had been leaning, I thought I could make out the name of Drablow: the letters were encrusted with a salt deposit blown, I suppose, off the estuary over years of bad winter weather.

In L . . . g Mem . . .
. . . net Drablow
. . . 190 . . .
. . . nd of He . . .
. . . iel . . . low
Bor . . .

I remembered that Mr Jerome had hinted at some Drablow family graves, no longer used, in a place other than the church-yard and supposed that this was the resting place of ancestors from years back. But it was quite certain that there was nothing and no one except old bones here now and I felt quite unafraid and tran-quil as I stood there, contemplating the scene and the place which had previously struck me as eerie, sinister, evil, but which now, I saw, was merely somewhat melancholy because it was so tumble-down and unfrequented. It was the sort of spot where, a hundred years or more earlier, romantically minded poets would have lin-gered and been inspired to compose some cloyingly sad verse.

I returned to the house with the dog, for already the air was turning much colder, the sky losing its light as the sun declined.

Indoors, I made myself some more tea and built up the fires and, before settling down again to those dull, dull papers, browsed at random among the bookshelves in the drawing room and chose myself some reading matter for later that evening, a novel by Sir Walter Scott and a volume of John Clare's poetry. These I took upstairs and placed on the locker of the small bedroom I had cho-sen to appropriate, mainly because it was at the front of the house but not so large and cold as the others and therefore, I thought, it would probably be cosier. From the window I could see the sec-tion of marsh away from the estuary and, if I craned my neck, the line of Nine Lives Causeway.

As I worked on into the evening, it grew dark, so I lit every lamp I could find, drew curtains and fetched in more coal and wood for the fires from a bunker in an outhouse I had located outside the scullery door.

The pile of waste paper grew in the box, by contrast with the few packets I thought ought to be examined more closely, and I fetched other boxes and drawersful from about the house. At this rate I should be through by the end of another day and a half at the most. I had a glass of sherry and a rather limited but not unpleasant supper which I shared with Spider and then, being tired of work, took a final turn outside before locking up.

All was quiet, there was not the slightest breeze. I could scarcely hear even the creeping of the water. Every bird had long since hidden for the night. The marshes were black and silent, stretching away from me for miles.

I have recounted the events — or rather, the non-events — of that day at Eel Marsh House in as much detail as I remember, in order to remind myself that I was in a calm and quite unexcitable state of mind. And that the odd events which had so frightened and unnerved me were all but forgotten. If I thought of them at all, it was mentally, as it were, to shrug my shoulders. Nothing else had happened, no harm had befallen me. The tenor of the day and the evening had been even, uninteresting, ordinary. Spider was an excellent companion and I was glad of the sound of her gentle breathing, her occasional scratching or clattering about, in that big, empty old house. But my main sensation was one of tedium and a certain lethargy, combined with a desire to finish the job and be back in London with my dear Stella. I remembered that I meant to tell her that we should get a small dog, as like Spider as possible, once we had a house of our own. Indeed, I decided to ask Mr Samuel Daily that if there were ever a chance of Spider having a litter of puppies he should reserve one for me.

I had worked assiduously and with concentration and taken some fresh air and exercise. For half an hour or so after retiring to bed I read *The Heart of Midlothian*, the dog settled on a rug at the foot of my bed. I think I must have fallen asleep only a few moments after putting the lamp out and slept quite deeply too, for when I awoke — or was awakened — very suddenly, I felt somewhat stunned, uncertain, for a second or two, where I was and why. I saw that it was quite dark but once my eyes were fully focused I saw the moonlight coming in through the window, for I had left the rather heavy, thick-looking curtains undrawn and the window slightly ajar. The moon fell upon the embroidered

counterpane and on the dark wood of wardrobe and chest and mirror with a cold, but rather beautiful light, and I thought that I would get out of bed and look at the marshes and the estuary from the window.

At first, all seemed very quiet, very still, and I wondered why I had awoken. Then, with a missed heart beat, I realised that Spider was up and standing at the door. Every hair of her body was on end, her ears were pricked, her tail erect, the whole of her tense, as if ready to spring. And she was emitting a soft, low growl from deep in her throat. I sat up paralysed, frozen, in the bed, conscious only of the dog and of the prickling of my own skin and of what suddenly seemed a different kind of silence, ominous and dreadful. And then, from somewhere within the depths of the house — but somewhere not very far from the room in which I was — I heard a noise. It was a faint noise, and, strain my ears as I might,

I could not make out exactly what it was. It was a sound like a regular yet intermittent bump or rumble. Nothing else happened. There were no footsteps, no creaking floorboards, the air was absolutely still, the wind did not moan through the casement. Only the muffled noise went on and the dog continued to stand, bristling at the door, now putting her nose to the gap at the bottom and snuffling along, now taking a pace backwards, head cocked and, like me, listening, listening. And, every so often, she growled again.

In the end, I suppose because nothing else happened and because I did have the dog to take with me, I managed to get out of bed, though I was shaken and my heart beat uncomfortably fast within me. But it took some time for me to find sufficient reserves of courage to enable me to open the bedroom door and stand out in the dark corridor. The moment I did so, Spider shot ahead and I heard her padding about, sniffing intently at every closed door, still growling and grumbling down in her throat.

After a while, I heard the odd sound again. It seemed to be coming from along the passage to my left, at the far end. But it was still quite impossible to identify. Very cautiously, listening, hardly breathing, I ventured a few steps in that direction. Spider went ahead of me. The passage led only to three other bedrooms on either side and, one by one, regaining my nerve as I went, I opened them and looked inside each one. Nothing, only heavy old furniture and empty unmade beds and, in the rooms at the back of the house, moonlight. Down below me on the ground floor of the house, silence, a seething, blanketing, almost tangible silence, and a musty darkness, thick as felt.

And then I reached the door at the very end of the passage. Spider was there before me and her body, as she sniffed beneath it, went rigid, her growling grew louder. I put my hand on her collar, stroked the rough, short hair, as much for my own reassurance as for hers. I could feel the tension in her limbs and body and it answered to my own.

This was the door without a keyhole, which I had been unable to open on my first visit to Eel Marsh House. I had no idea what was beyond it. Except the sound. It was coming from within that room, not very loud but just to hand, on the other side of that single wooden partition. It was a sound of something bumping gently on the floor, in a rhythmic sort of way, a familiar sort of sound and yet one I still could not exactly place, a sound that seemed to belong to my past, to waken old, half-forgotten memories and associations deep within me, a sound that, in any other place, would not have made me afraid but would, I thought, have been curiously comforting, friendly.

But, at my feet, the dog Spider began to whine, a thin, pitiful, frightened moan, and to back away from the door a little and press against my legs. My throat felt constricted and dry and I had begun to shiver. There was something in that room and I could not get to it, nor would I dare to, if I were able. I told myself it was a rat or a trapped bird, fallen down the chimney into the hearth and unable to get out again. But the sound was not that of some small, panic-stricken creature. Bump bump. Pause. Bump bump. Pause. Bump bump. Bump bump. Bump bump.

I think that I might have stood there, in bewilderment and terror, all night, or else taken to my heels, with the dog, and run out of the house altogether, had I not heard another, faint sound. It came from behind me, not directly behind but from the front of the house. I turned away from the locked door and went back, shakily, groping along the wall to my bedroom, guided by the slant of moonlight that reached out into the darkness of the corridor. The dog was half a pace ahead of me.

There was nothing in the room at all, the bed was as I had left it, there had been no disturbances; then I realised that the sounds had been coming not from within the room but outside it, beyond the window. I pulled it up as far as the sash would allow and looked out. There lay the marshes, silver-grey and empty, there was the water of the estuary, flat as a mirror with the full moon lying upturned upon it. Nothing. No one. Except, like a wash from far, far away, so that I half wondered if I were remembering and reliving the memory, a cry, a child's cry. But no. The slightest of breezes stirred the surface of the water, wrinkling it, and passing dryly through the reed beds and away. Nothing more.

I felt something warm against my ankle and, looking down,

saw that it was Spider, very close to me and gently licking my skin. When I stroked her, I realised that she was calm again, her body relaxed, her ears down. I listened. There was no sound in the house at all. After a while, I went back along the passage to the closed door. Spider came quite happily and stood obediently there, perhaps waiting for the door to be opened. I put my head close to the wood. Nothing. Absolute silence. I put my hand on the door handle, hesitated as I felt my heart again begin to race, but drew in several deep breaths and tried the door. It would not open, though the rattling of it echoed in the room beyond, as if there were no carpet on the floor. I tried it once more and pushed against it slightly with my shoulder. It did not give.

In the end I went back to bed. I read two further chapters of the Scott novel, though without fully taking in their meaning, and then switched out my lamp. Spider had settled again on the rug. It was a little after two o'clock.

It was a long time before I slept.

The first thing I noticed on the following morning was a change in the weather. As soon as I awoke, a little before seven, I felt that the air had a dampness in it and that it was rather colder and, when I looked out of the window, I could hardly see the division between land and water, water and sky, all was a uniform grey, with thick cloud lying low over the marsh and a drizzle. It was not a day calculated to raise the spirits and I felt unrefreshed and nervous after the previous night. But Spider trotted down the stairs eagerly and cheerfully enough and I soon built up the fires again and stoked the boiler, had a bath and breakfast and began to feel more like my everyday self. I even went back upstairs and along the corridor to the door of the locked room, but there was no strange sound from within, no sound at all.

At nine o'clock I went out, taking the bicycle and pedalling hard, to work up a good head of speed across the causeway and through the country lanes back to Crythin, with Spider bounding behind me and taking off every so often, to burrow briefly in a ditch or start after some creature that flitted away across the fields.

I had the landlord's wife refill my hamper with plenty of food and bought more from the grocer's. With both of them and with Mr Jerome, whom I met in a side street, I spoke briefly and jestingly and I said nothing whatsoever about the business at Eel Marsh House. Daylight, even such a dreary damp affair as it was, had once again renewed my nerve and resolve and banished the vapours of the night. Moreover, there was a fond letter from Stella, full of gratifying exclamations of regret at my absence and pride in my new responsibility, and it was with this warming my inside pocket that I cycled back towards the marshes and the house, whistling as I went.

Although it was not yet lunchtime I was obliged to put on most of the lamps in the house, for the day lowered, and the light was too poor to work by, even directly in front of the window. Looking out, I saw that the cloud and drizzle had thickened, so that I could scarcely see beyond the grass that ran down to the edges of the water and, as the afternoon began to draw in, they had merged together to form a fog. Then my nerve began to falter a little and I decided I might pack up and return to the comfort of the town. I went to the front door and stepped out. At once the dampness clung to my face and to my clothes like a fine web. There was a stronger wind now, whipping off the estuary and going through to my bones, with its raw coldness. Spider ran off a yard or two and then stopped and looked back at me, uncertain, not anxious to walk far in such dreary weather. I could not see the ruin or the walls of the old burial ground, away across the field, the low-lying cloud and mist had blotted them out. Neither could I see the causeway path, not only because of that but because the tide had now covered it over completely. It would be late at night before it was clear again. I could not retreat to Crythin Gifford after all.

I whistled the dog, who came at once and gladly, and returned to Mrs Drablow's papers. So far I had found only one interesting-looking, slim packet of documents and letters, and I decided that I would give myself the possible diversion of reading them that evening after supper. Until then I cleared several more piles of rubbish and was cheered by the sight of the several now-empty boxes and drawers, depressed by those that still remained full and unsifted.

The first packet of letters, bundled together and tied with narrow purple ribbon, were all written in the same hand, between a February of about sixty years before and the summer of the following year. They were sent first from the manor house of a village I remembered from the map as being some twenty miles away from Crythin Gifford, and later from a lodge in the Scottish countryside beyond Edinburgh. All were addressed to 'My dear' or 'Dearest Alice' and signed for the most part 'J' but occasionally 'Jennet'. They were short letters, written in a direct, rather naive manner, and the story they told was a touching one and not particularly unfamiliar. The writer, a young woman and apparently a relative of Mrs Drablow, was unmarried and with child. At first, she was still living at home, with her parents; later, she was sent away. Scarcely any mention was made of the child's father, except for a couple of references to P. 'P will not come back here.' And: 'I think P was sent abroad.' In Scotland, a son was born to her and she wrote of him at once with a desperate, clinging affection. For a few months the letters ceased, but when they began again it was at first in passionate outrage and protest, later, in quiet, resigned bitterness. Pressure was being exerted upon her to give up the child for adoption; she refused, saying over and over again that they would 'never be parted'.

'He is mine. Why should I not have what is mine? He shall not go to strangers. I shall kill us both before I let him go.'

Then the tone changed.

'What else can I do? I am quite helpless. If you and M are to have him I shall mind it less.' And again, 'I suppose it must be.'

But at the end of the last letter of all was written in a very small, cramped hand: 'Love him, take care of him as your own. But he is mine, mine, he can *never* be yours. Oh, forgive me. I think my heart will break. J.'

In the same packet, there was a simple document drawn up by a lawyer, declaring that Nathaniel Pierston, infant son of Jennet Humfrye, was become by adoption the child of Morgan Thomas Drablow of Eel Marsh House, Crythin Gifford, and of his wife Alice. Attached to this were three other papers. The first was a reference from a Lady M — in Hyde Park Gate — for a nursemaid called Rose Judd.

I had read and set this aside, and was about to open the next, a single folded sheet, when I looked up suddenly, startled into the present by a noise.

Spider was at the door, growling the same, low growl of the previous night. I looked round at her and saw that her hackles were up. For a moment I sat, too terrified to move. Then I recalled my decision to seek out the ghosts of Eel Marsh House and confront them, for I was sure — or I had been sure, in the hours of daylight — that the harder I ran away from those things, the closer they would come after me and dog my heels, and the greater would be their power to disturb me. And so, I laid down the papers, got to my feet and went quietly to open the door of the small parlour in which I had been sitting.

At once, Spider shot out of the room as though after a hare and made for the staircase, still growling. I heard her scurry along the passage above and then stop. She had gone to the locked door and even from below I could hear it again, the odd, faint, rhythmic noise — bump bump, pause, bump bump, pause, bump bump. . .

Determined to break in if I possibly could, and to identify the noise and whatever was making it, I went into the kitchen and scullery, in search of a strong hammer or chisel or other forcing tool. But, not finding anything there and remembering that there was a wood axe in the outhouse where the fuel was stored, I opened the back door and, taking my torch with me, stepped outside.

There was still a mist and a drizzling dampness in the air, though nothing like the dense, swirling fog of the night when I had crossed the causeway path. But it was pitch dark: there was neither moonlight nor any stars visible and I stumbled about on my way to the shed in spite of the beam from my torch.

It was when I had located the axe and was making my way back to the house that I heard the noise and, when I heard it, so close that I thought it was only a few yards from the house, turned back, instead of going in, walked quickly around to the front door, expecting to greet a visitor.

As I came onto the gravel, I shone my torch out into the darkness in the direction of the causeway path. It was from there that the clip clop of the pony's hooves and the rumbling and creaking of the trap was coming. But I could see nothing. And then, with an awful cry of realisation, I knew. There was no visitor or at least no real, human visitor — no Keckwick. The noise was beginning to come from a different direction now, as the pony and trap left the causeway and struck off across the open marsh.

I stood, hideously afraid, straining into the murky, misty distance with my ears, to try and detect any difference between this sound and that of a real vehicle. But there was none. If I could have run out of there, seen my way, I must surely have been able to reach it, climb up onto it, challenge its driver. As it was, I could do nothing but stand, stand as still and stiff as a post, rigid with fear and yet inwardly in a turmoil of nervous apprehension and imaginings and responses.

Then I realised that the dog had come down and was beside me on the gravel, her body absolutely still, ears pricked, facing the marsh and the source. The pony trap was going further away now, the noise of its wheels was becoming muffled and then there was the sound of splashing water and churning mud, the noise of the pony plunging about in terror. It was happening, the whole thing was caught up in the quicksands and sinking, sinking, there was a terrible moment when the waters began to close around it and to gurgle, and then, above it all, and above the whinnying and struggling of the pony, the child's cry, that rose and rose to a scream of terror and was then slowly choked and drowned; and, finally, silence.

Then nothing, save the lap and eddy of the water far away. My whole body was trembling, my mouth dry, the palms of my hands sore where I had dug my nails into them as I had stood, helplessly, hearing that dreadful sequence of sounds repeated again, as it would be repeated in my head a thousand times forever after.

That the pony and trap and the crying child were not real I had no shadow of a doubt, that their final drive across the marshes and their disappearance into the treacherous quicksands had not just taken place a hundred yards away from me in the darkness, of this I was now certain. But I was equally certain that once, who knew how long ago, but one actual day, this dreadful thing had indeed taken place, here on Eel Marsh. A pony and trap with whoever was its driver, together with a child passenger, had been swallowed up and drowned within a few moments. At the very thought of it, let alone at this awful ghostly repetition of the whole event, I was more distressed than I could bear. I stood shivering, cold from the mist and the night wind and from the sweat that was rapidly cooling on my body.

And then, hair bristling, with eyes a-start, the dog Spider took a couple of steps backwards, half lifted her front paws off the ground and began to howl, a loud, prolonged, agonised and heart-stopping howl.

In the end, I had to lift her up and carry her inside the house — she would not move in answer to any call. Her body was stiff in my arms and she was clearly in a state of distress, and, when I set her down on the floor of the hall, she clung close to my heels.

In a curious way, it was her fearfulness that persuaded me that I must retain control of myself, rather as a mother will feel obliged to put a brave face on things in order to calm her frightened child. Spider was only a dog but nevertheless I felt obliged to soothe and reassure her, and, in doing so, was able to calm myself and gather some inner strength. But, after a few moments of allowing herself to be stroked and petted under my hand, the dog broke away and, alert again and growling, made for the stairs. I followed her quickly, switching on every light I could find as I went. As I expected, she had made for the passage, with the locked door at the end of it, and already I could hear the noise, that maddeningly familiar bump that tantalised me because I still could not identify it.

I was breathing fast as I ran to the corner and my heart seemed to be leaping about madly within me. But, if I had been afraid at what had happened in this house so far, when I reached the end of the short corridor and saw what I did see now, my fear reached a new height, until for a minute I thought I would die of it, *was* dying, for I could not conceive of a man's being able to endure such shocks and starts and remain alive, let alone in his right senses.

The door of the room from which the noise came, the door which had been securely locked, so that I had not been able to break it down, the door to which there could not be a key — that door was now standing open. Wide open.

Beyond it lay a room, in complete darkness, save for the first yard or two immediately at the entrance, where the dim light from the bulb on the landing outside fell onto some shining, brown floor covering. Within, I could hear both the noise — louder now because the door was open — and the sound of the dog, pattering anxiously about and sniffing and snuffling as she went.

I do not know how long I stood there in fear and trembling and in dreadful bewilderment. I lost all sense of time and ordinary reality. Through my head went a tumbling confusion of half thoughts and emotions, visions of spectres and of real fleshy intruders, ideas of murder and violence, and all manner of odd, distorted fears. And, all the time, the door stood wide open and the rocking continued. Rocking. Yes. I came to, because I had realised at last what the noise within the room was — or, at least, what it reminded me of closely. It was the sound of the wooden runners of my nurse's rocking chair, when she had sat beside me every night while I went to sleep, as a small child, rocking, rocking. Sometimes, when I was ill and feverish or had wakened from the throes of some nightmare, she or my mother had come to me and lifted me out of my bed and sat with me in that same chair, holding me and rocking until I was soothed and sleepy again. The sound that I had been hearing was the sound that I remembered from far back, from a time before I could clearly remember anything else. It was the sound that meant comfort and safety, peace and reassurance, the regular, rhythmical sound at the end of the day, that lulled me asleep and into my dreams, the sound that meant that one of the two people in the world to whom I was closest and whom I most loved was nearby. And so, as I stood there in that dark passageway, listening, the sound began to exert the same effect upon me now until I felt hypnotised by it into a state of drowsiness and rest; my fears and the tensions in my body they had aroused began to slip away, I was breathing slowly and more deeply and felt a warmth creeping into my limbs. I felt that nothing could come near to harm or affright me, but I had a protector and guardian close at hand. And, indeed, perhaps I had, perhaps all I had ever learned and believed in the nursery about unseen heavenly spirits surrounding, upholding and preserving us was indeed true; or perhaps it was only that my memories aroused by the rocking sound were so positive and so

powerfully strong that they overcame and quite drove out all that
was sinister and alarming, evil and disturbed.

Whichever might be the case, I knew that I now had courage
enough to go into that room and face whatever might be there
and so, before the conviction faltered, and my fears could return,
I walked in, as determinedly and boldly and firmly as I could. As I
did so I put my hand up to the light switch on the wall but when
I pressed it no illumination came and, shining my torch onto the
ceiling, I saw that the socket was bare of any light bulb. But the
beam from my own lamp was quite strong and bright, it gave me
ample light for my purpose and now, as I went into the room,
Spider gave a low whine from one corner, but did not come over
to me. Very slowly and cautiously I looked around the room.

It was almost the room I had just been remembering, the room to which the sound I had identified belonged. It was a child's nursery. There was the bed in one corner, the same sort of low, narrow wooden bed that I myself had once slept in, and beside it and facing the open fireplace at an angle stood the rocking chair and that too was the same or very similar, a low-seated, tall, ladder-backed chair made of dark wood — elm, perhaps, and with wide, worn, curved runners. As I watched, stared until I could stare no harder, it rocked gently and with gradually decreasing speed, in the way any such chair will continue to rock for a time after someone has just got out of it.

But no one had been there. The room had been empty. Anyone who had just left it must have come out into the corridor and confronted me, I would have had to move aside to let them pass.

I shone the torch rapidly all around the wall. There was the chimney breast and fireplace, there was the window closed and bolted and with two wooden bars across it, such as all nurseries have to guard the children from falling out; there was no other door.

Gradually the chair rocked less and less, until the movements were so slight I could scarcely see or hear them. Then they stopped and there was absolute silence.

The nursery was fully furnished and equipped and in such good order that the occupant of it might only have gone away for a night or two or even simply taken a walk, there was none of the damp, bare, unlived-in feeling of all the other rooms of Eel Marsh House. Carefully and cautiously, almost holding my breath, I explored it. I looked at the bed, made up and all complete with sheets and pillows, blankets and counterpane. Beside it was a small table and on the table a tiny wooden horse and a night-light with the candle half burnt away, still in place and with water in the holder. In the chest of drawers and wardrobe there were clothes, underclothes, day clothes, formal clothes, play clothes, clothes for a small boy of six or seven years old, beautiful, well-made clothes, in the style of those which my own parents wore as children in those formal photographs we still have about the house, the styles of sixty years or more ago.

And then there were the child's toys, so many toys and all of them most neatly and meticulously ordered and cared for. There were rows of lead soldiers, arranged in regiments, and a farm, set out with painted barns and fences, haycocks and little wooden stooks of corn and on a big board. There was a model ship complete with masts and sails of linen, yellowed a little by age, and a whip with a leather thong, lying beside a polished spinning top. There were games of ludo and halma, draughts and chess, there were jigsaw puzzles of country scenes and circuses and the 'Boyhood of Raleigh', and in a small wooden chest there was a monkey made of leather and a cat and four kittens knitted from wool, a furry bear and a bald doll with a china head and a sailor suit. The child had had pens and brushes, too, and bottles of coloured inks and a book of nursery rhymes and another of Greek stories and a bible and a prayer book, a set of dice and two packs of playing cards, a miniature trumpet and a painted musical box from Switzerland and a Black Sambo made of tin with jointed arms and legs.

I picked things up, stroked them, even smelled them. They must have been here for half a century, yet they might have been played with this afternoon and tidied away tonight. I was not afraid now. I was puzzled. I felt strange, unlike myself, I moved as if in a dream. But for the moment at least there was nothing here to frighten or harm me, there was only emptiness, an open door, a neatly made bed and a curious air of sadness, of something lost, missing, so that I myself felt a desolation, a grief in my own heart. How can I explain? I cannot. But I remember it, as I felt it.

The dog was sitting quietly now on the rag rug beside the child's bed and in the end, because I had examined everything and could not explain any of it and did not want to be in that sad atmosphere any longer, I went out, after taking a last slow look around, closing the door behind me.

It was not late but I had no more energy left to go on reading Mrs Drablow's papers, I felt drained, exhausted, all the emotions that had poured into me and out again leaving me like something thrown up on a calm beach at the end of a storm.

I made myself a drink of hot water and brandy and did my round of the house, banking up the fires and locking the doors, before going to bed, to read Sir Walter Scott.

Whistle and I'll Come to You

DURING THE NIGHT the wind rose. As I had lain reading I had become aware of the stronger gusts that blew every so often against the casements. But when I awoke abruptly in the early hours it had increased greatly in force. The house felt like a ship at sea, battered by the gale that came roaring across the open marsh. Windows were rattling everywhere and there was the sound of moaning down all the chimneys of the house and whistling through every nook and cranny.

At first I was alarmed. Then, as I lay still, gathering my wits, I reflected on how long Eel Marsh House had stood here, steady as a lighthouse, quite alone and exposed, bearing the brunt of winter after winter of gales and driving rain and sleet and spray. It was unlikely to blow away tonight. And then, those memories of childhood began to be stirred again and I dwelt nostalgically upon all those nights when I had lain in the warm and snug safety of my bed in the nursery at the top of our family house in Sussex, hearing the wind rage round like a lion, howling at the doors and beating upon the windows but powerless to reach me. I lay back and slipped into that pleasant, trance-like state somewhere between sleeping and waking, recalling the past and all its emotions and impressions vividly, until I felt I was a small boy again.

Then from somewhere, out of that howling darkness, a cry came to my ears, catapulting me back into the present and banishing all tranquillity.

I listened hard. Nothing. The tumult of the wind, like a banshee, and the banging and rattling of the window in its old, ill-fitting frame. Then yes, again, a cry, that familiar cry of desperation and anguish, a cry for help from a child somewhere out on the marsh.

There was no child. I knew that. How could there be? Yet how could I lie here and ignore even the crying of some long-dead ghost?

'Rest in peace', I thought, but this poor one did not, could not.

After a few moments I got up. I would go down into the kitchen and make myself a drink, stir up the fire a little and sit beside it trying, trying to shut out that calling voice for which I could do nothing, and no one had been able to do anything for . . . how many years?

As I went out onto the landing, Spider the dog following me at once, two things happened together. I had the impression of someone who had just that very second before gone past me on their way from the top of the stairs to one of the other rooms, and, as a tremendous blast of wind hit the house so that it all but seemed to rock at the impact, the lights went out. I had not bothered to pick up my torch from the bedside table and now I stood in the pitch blackness, unsure for a moment of my bearings.

And the person who had gone by, and who was now in this house with me? I had seen no one, felt nothing. There had been no movement, no brush of a sleeve against mine, no disturbance of the air, I had not even heard a footstep. I had simply the absolutely certain sense of someone just having passed close to me and gone away down the corridor. Down the short narrow corridor that led to the nursery whose door had been so firmly locked and then, inexplicably, opened.

For a moment, I actually began to conjecture that there was indeed someone — another human being — living here in this house, a person who hid themselves away in that mysterious nursery and came out at night to fetch food and drink and to take the air. Perhaps it was the woman in black? Had Mrs Drablow harboured some reclusive old sister or retainer, had she left behind her a mad friend that no one had known about? My brain spun all manner of wild, incoherent fantasies as I tried desperately to provide a rational explanation for the presence I had been so aware of. But then they ceased. There was no living occupant of Eel Marsh House other than myself and Samuel Daily's dog. Whatever was about, whoever I had seen, and heard rocking, and who had passed me by just now, whoever had opened the locked door was not 'real'. No. But what *was* 'real'? At that moment I began to doubt my own reality.

The first thing I must have was a light and I groped my way back across to my bed, reached over it and got my hand to the torch at last, took a step back, stumbled over the dog who was at my heels and dropped the torch. It went spinning away across the floor and fell somewhere by the window with a crash and the faint sound of breaking glass. I cursed but managed, by crawling about on my hands and knees, to find it again and to press the switch. No light came on. The torch had broken.

For a moment I was as near to weeping tears of despair and fear, frustration and tension, as I had ever been since my child-hood. But instead of crying I drummed my fists upon the floor-boards, in a burst of violent rage, until they throbbed.

It was Spider who brought me to my senses by scratching a lit-tle at my arm and then by licking the hand I stretched out to her. We sat on the floor together and I hugged her warm body to me, glad of her, thoroughly ashamed of myself, calmer and relieved, while the wind boomed and roared without, and again and again I heard that child's terrible cry borne on the gusts towards me.

I would not sleep again, of that I was sure, but nor did I dare to go down the stairs in that utter darkness, surrounded by the noise of the storm, unnerved by the awareness I had had of the presence of that other one. My torch was broken. I must have a candle, some light, however faint and frail, to keep me company. There was a candle near at hand. I had seen it earlier, on the table beside the small bed in the nursery.

For a very long time, I could not summon up sufficient courage to grope my way along that short passage to the room which I realised was somehow both the focus and the source of all the strange happenings in the house. I was lost to everything but my own fears, incapable of decisive, coherent thought, let alone movement. But gradually I discovered for myself the truth of the axiom that a man cannot remain indefinitely in a state of active terror. Either the emotion will increase until, at the prompting of more and more dreadful events and apprehensions, he is so over-come by it that he runs away or goes mad; or he will become by slow degrees less agitated and more in possession of himself.

The wind continued to howl across the marshes and batter at the house but that was, after all, a natural sound and one that I could recognise and tolerate, for it could not hurt me in any way. And the darkness did not brighten and would not for some hours but there is no more in the simple state of darkness itself to make a man afraid than in the sound of a storm wind. Nothing else happened at all. All sense of another one's presence had faded away, the faint cries of the child ceased at last and from the nurs-ery at the end of the passage came not the faintest sound of the rocking chair or of any other movement. I had prayed, as I had crouched on the floor boards with the dog clutched to me, prayed that whatever had disturbed me and was within the house should be banished or at least that I should gain possession of myself enough to confront and overcome it.

Now, as I got to my feet unsteadily, aching and stiff in every limb, so great had been the tension of my body, I did at last feel able to make some move, though I was profoundly relieved that, so far as I could tell, there was, for the moment at least, nothing worse to face up to than my blind journey down the corridor to the nursery, in search of the candle.

That journey I made, very slowly and in mounting trepidation but successfully, for I found my way to the bedside and took up the candle in its holder and, grasping it tightly, began to fumble with my hand along the walls and the furniture, back towards the door.

I have said that there were no other strange and dreadful hap-penings that night, nothing else to make me afraid except the sound of the wind and the completeness of the dark, and in a sense that is true, for the nursery was quite empty and the rocking chair still and silent, all, so far as I could tell, was as it had been before. I did not know then to what I could possibly attribute the feelings that swept over me from the moment I entered the room. I felt not fear, not horror, but an overwhelming grief and sadness, a sense of loss and bereavement, a distress mingled with utter despair. My parents were both alive, I had one brother, a good many friends and my fiancée, Stella. I was still a young man. Apart from the inevitable loss of elderly aunts and uncles and grandparents I had never experienced the death of anyone close to me, never truly mourned and suffered the extremes of grief. Never yet. But the feelings that must accompany the death of someone as close to my heart and bound up with my own being as it was possible to be, I knew then, in the nursery of Eel Marsh House. They all but broke me, yet I was confused and puzzled, not knowing any reason at all why I should be in the grip of such desperate anguish and misery. It was as though I had, for the time that I was in the room, become another person, or at least experienced the emotions that belong to another.

It was as alarming and strange an occurrence as any of those more outward, visible and audible that had taken place over these past few days.

When I left the room and closed the door behind me and stood in the corridor again, the feelings dropped away from me like a garment that had been put over my shoulders for a short time and then removed again. I was back within my own person, my own emotions, I was myself again.

I returned unsteadily to my bedroom, found the matches that I kept in my coat pocket along with my pipe and tobacco and lit the candle at last. As I gripped the hoop of the tin holder in my fingers my hand trembled so that the yellow flame flickered and swerved about, reflecting here and there crazily upon walls and door, floor and ceiling, mirror and counterpane. But it was a comfort and a relief nonetheless and in the end it burned brightly and well, as I became less agitated.

I saw the face of my watch. It was barely three o'clock and I hoped that the candle would burn until dawn, which on a stormy day at this fag end of the year would come late.

I sat up in bed, wrapped in my coat, and read Sir Walter Scott as best I could by the meagre flame. Whether it went out before the first thin grey light sneaked into the room I do not know, for in the end and without meaning to do so I fell asleep. When I awoke it was into a watery, washed-out dawn, I was uncomfortable and stale, the candle had burned to the last drop of wax and guttered out, leaving only a black stain at its base, and my book was fallen onto the floor.

Once again it was a noise that had awakened me. Spider was scratching and whining at the door and I realised that it was some hours since the poor creature had been let out. I got up and dressed briskly, went downstairs and opened the front door. The sky was swollen and streaked with rain clouds, everything looked drab and without colour and the estuary was running high. But the wind had died down, the air was lighter and very cold.

At first the dog trotted across the gravel towards the scrubby grass, anxious to relieve herself, while I stood yawning, trying to get some life and warmth into my body by beating my arms and

stamping my feet. I decided that I would put on a coat and boots and go for a brisk walk across the field, to clear my head, and was turning to go back into the house when, from far out on the marshes, I heard, unmistakably clean and clear, the sound of someone whistling, as one whistles to summon a dog.

Spider stopped dead in her tracks for a split second and then, before I could restrain her, before I had fully gathered my wits, she set off, as though after a hare, running low and fast away from the house, away from the safety of the grass and out across the wet marshes. For a few moments I stood amazed and bewildered and could not move, only stared as Spider's small form receded into that great open expanse. I could see no one out there, but the whistle had been real, not a trick of the wind. Yet I would have sworn it had not come from any human lips. Then, even as I looked, I saw the dog falter and slow down and finally stop and I realised in horror that she was floundering in mud, fighting to maintain her balance

from the pull beneath her feet. I ran as I have never run before, heedless of my own safety, desperate to go to the aid of the brave, bright little creature who had given me such consolation and cheer in that desolate spot.

At first the path was firm, though muddy, beneath my feet and I could make good speed. The wind coming across the estuary was bitingly cold on my face and I felt my eyes begin to smart and water, so that I had to wipe them in order to see my way clearly. Spider was yelping loudly now, afraid but still visible, and I called to her, trying to reassure her. Then I, too, began to feel the stickiness and the unsteadiness of the ground as it became boggier. Once I plunged my leg down and it stuck fast in a watery hole until I managed to exert all my strength and get free. All around me the water was swollen and murky, the tide of the estuary was now high, running across the marshes themselves, and I was obliged to wade rather than walk. But at last, out of breath and straining with every movement I got almost within reach of the dog. She could scarcely hold up now, her legs and half her body had disappeared beneath the whirling, sucking bog and her pointed head was held up in the air as she struggled and yelped all the while. I tried two or three times to stride across to her but each time I had to pull free abruptly for fear of going under myself. I wished that I had got a stick to throw across to her, as some sort of grappling hook with which to grab hold of her collar. I felt a second of pure despair, alone in the middle of the wide marsh, under the fast-moving, stormy sky, with only water all around me and that dreadful house the only solid thing for miles around.

But aware that, if I gave in to panic, I should most certainly be lost, I thought furiously and then, very cautiously, lay down full length on the marsh mud, keeping my lower body pressed as hard as I could onto a small island of solid ground and, reaching and stretching my trunk and my arms forward, inch by inch, gasping for breath until, just as the last of her body sank, I lunged out and grabbed the dog about the neck and hauled and strained and tugged with all the force I could, a strength I would never have dreamed I could have summoned up, born of terror and desperation; and after an agonising time, when we both fought for our lives against that treacherous quicksand that tried to pull us both down into itself and I felt my grip on the slippery wet fur and wet flesh of the dog almost give, at last I knew that I would hold and win. I strained as hard as ever I could to drag my body backwards onto firmer ground. As I did so, the dog's body suddenly gave and the tug of war was over as I fell back, holding her tight, the two of us soaked with water and mud, my chest burning and my lungs almost bursting, my arms feeling as if they had been dragged from their sockets, as indeed they almost had.

We rested, panting, exhausted, and I wondered if I would ever be able to get up, I felt suddenly so faint and weak and lost in the middle of the marsh. The poor dog was making choking noises now and rubbing her head against me over and over, no doubt both terrified and also in great pain, for I had nearly asphyxiated her as I had clutched so hard around her neck. But she was alive and so was I and, gradually, a little warmth from each of our bodies and the pause revived us and, cradling Spider like a child in my arms, I began to stumble back across the marshes towards the house. As I did so and within a few yards of it, I glanced up. At one of the upper windows, the only window with bars across it, the window of the nursery, I caught a glimpse of someone standing. A woman. That woman. She was looking directly towards me.

Spider was whimpering in my arms and making occasional little retching coughs. We were both trembling violently. How I reached the grass in front of the house I shall never know but, as I did so, I heard a sound. It was coming from the far end of the causeway path which was just beginning to be visible as the tide began to recede. It was the sound of a pony trap.

A Packet of Letters

THERE WAS a bright light and I was staring into it — or, rather, I felt that *it* was boring into *me*, boring through my eyes right into my brain and I struggled to turn my head away and my head seemed to be very light, scarcely set on my shoulders at all, but spinning, floating like blown thistledown!

Then abruptly the light was removed and when I opened my eyes the normal world and ordinary things in it came into focus again. I found myself lying, propped up on the couch in the morning room, with the large, red, concerned face of Mr Samuel Daily looming over me. In his hand he held a pocket torch, with which, I realised, he must have been peering into my eyes, in a crude attempt to arouse me.

I sat up, but at once the walls began to shift and buckle forward and I was obliged to lie back again weakly. And then, in a rush, everything came back to me with great force, the chase after the dog across the wet marshes and the struggle to free her, the sight of the woman in black at the nursery window and then those sounds which had caused my fears to mount to such a height that I had lost control of myself and my senses and fallen unconscious.

'But the trap — the pony and trap. . .'

'At the front door.'

I stared.

'Oh, I still like to make use of it now and again. It's a pleasant way to travel when there's nothing to hurry over and it's a sight safer than a motor-car across that causeway.'

'Ah.' I felt a surge of relief as I realised the plain facts of the matter, that the noise I had heard had been that of a real pony and cart.

'What did you think?' He was looking at me keenly.

'A pony and cart —'

'Yes?'

'I'd — heard others. Another.'

'Keckwick, perhaps,' he said evenly.

'No, no.' I sat up, more cautiously, and the room stayed firm.

'You take care now.'

'I'm better — I'm all right. It was. . .' I wiped my brow. 'I should like a drink.'

'At your elbow.'

I turned and saw a jug of water and a glass and I drank thirstily, beginning to feel more and more refreshed and my nerves to be steadier as I did so.

Realising it, Mr Daily moved away from my side to a chair opposite and sat himself down.

'I had you on my mind,' he said at last. 'I wasn't happy. It began to unsettle me.'

'Isn't it quite early in the morning — I've become confused. . .'

'Early enough. I kept waking. As I said, I had you on my mind.'

'How strange.'

'Was it? Not as it seems to me. Not strange at all.'

'No.'

'A good job I came when I did.'

'Yes, indeed, I'm very grateful. You must have — what? Carried me in here, I remember nothing about it.'

'I've dragged heavier than you with one arm around my neck — there's not much flesh on your bones.'

'I'm extremely glad to see you, Mr Daily.'

'You've good reason.'

'I have.'

'People have drowned on that marsh before now.'

'Yes. Yes, I know that now. I felt that I was being pulled under and the dog with me.' I started up. 'Spider. . .'

'She's here. She'll do.'

I looked to where he nodded, to the dog down on the rug between us. At the sound of her name, she bumped her tail, but otherwise she lay, the mud drying on her coat in clots and streaks, and pasted thickly to her leg, looking as limp and exhausted as I myself felt.

'Now, when you've come to a bit more, you'd better get whatever you need and we'll be off.'

'Off?'

'Ay. I came to see how you were faring in this godforsaken place. I have seen. You had better come back home with me and recover yourself.'

I did not answer for a few moments but lay back and went over in my mind the sequence of events of the previous night and of this morning — and, indeed, further back than that, from my first visit here. I knew that there had been hauntings by the woman in black and perhaps by some other occupant of this house. I knew that the sounds I had heard out on the marsh were ghostly sounds. But although these had been terrifying, and inexplicable, I thought that if I had to I could go over them again, if only because I had been growing more and more determined to find out what restless soul it was who wanted to cause these disturbances and why, *why*. If I could uncover the truth, perhaps I might in some way put an end to it all forever.

But what I couldn't endure more was the atmosphere surrounding the events: the sense of oppressive hatred and malevolence, of someone's evil and also of terrible grief and distress. These, which seemed to invade my own soul and take charge of me, these were what I could no longer bear. I told Mr Daily that I would be glad and grateful to go back with him and to rest at his house if only for a short while. But I was worried, not wanting to leave the mystery unexplained and knowing, too, that at the same time someone would have to finish, at some point, the necessary work of sorting out and packing up Mrs Drablow's papers.

This I mentioned now.

'And what have you found here, Mr Kipps? A map to buried treasure?'

'No. A great quantity of rubbish, old waste paper, and precious little of interest, let alone of value. Frankly, I doubt whether there will be anything. But the job will have to be done at some time or other. We are obliged to it.'

I got up and began to walk about the room, trying my limbs and finding them more or less steady.

'For now, I don't mind confessing that I shall be pretty glad to let up and leave the lot of it behind. There were just one or two papers I should like to go over again for my own curiosity. There is a packet of old letters with a few documents attached. I was reading them late last night. I shall bring those with me.'

Then, while Mr Daily began to go round the downstairs rooms, drawing the blinds, checking that all the fires were extinguished, I went first to the room in which I had been working to gather together the bundle of letters and then upstairs for my few belongings. I was no longer at all afraid because I was leaving Eel Marsh House at least for the time being and because of the large and reassuring presence of Mr Samuel Daily. Whether I would ever return here I did not know but certainly if I did so it would not be alone. I felt altogether calm, therefore, as I reached the top of the staircase and turned towards the small bedroom I had been using, the events of the previous night seeming far in the past and with no more power to harm me than a particularly bad nightmare.

I packed up my bag quickly, closed the window and drew down the blind. On the floor lay the remnants of the shattered torch and I swept them together into a corner with the edge of my foot. All was quiet now, the wind had been dropping since dawn, though, if I closed my eyes, I could hear again its moaning and crying and all the banging and rattling it had given rise to in the old house. But, although that had contributed to my nervousness, I could perfectly well sort out those incidental events — the storm, the bumps and creaks, the darkness, from the ghostly happenings and the atmosphere surrounding them. The weather might change, the wind drop, the sun shine, Eel Marsh House might stand quiet and still. It would be no less dreadful. Whoever haunted it and whatever terrible emotions still possessed them would continue to disturb and distress anyone who came near here, that I knew.

I finished picking up my belongings and left the room. As I reached the landing I could not prevent myself from glancing quickly and half-fearfully along the passage that led to the nursery.

The door was ajar. I stood, feeling the anxiety that lay only just below the surface begin to rise up within me, making my heart beat fast. Below, I heard Mr Daily's footsteps and the pitter-patter of the dog as it followed him about. And, reassured by their presence, I summoned up my courage and made my way cautiously towards that half-open door. When I reached it I hesitated. She had been there. I had seen her. Whoever she was, this was the focus of her search or her attention or her grief — I could not tell which. This was the very heart of the haunting.

There was no sound now. The rocking chair was still. Very slowly I pushed open the door wider and wider, inch by inch, and took a few steps forward until I could see all the way into the room.

It was in a state of disarray as might have been caused by a gang of robbers, bent on mad, senseless destruction. Whereas the bed had been made up neatly, now the clothes were pulled off anyhow and bundled up or trailing onto the floor. The wardrobe door and the drawers of the small chest were pulled open and all the clothes they contained half-dragged out, and left hanging like entrails from a wounded body. The lead soldiers had been knocked down like a set of ninepins and the wooden animals from the ark strewn about the shelf, books lay open, their jackets torn, puzzles and games were all jumbled up in a heap together in the centre of the floor. Soft toys were split and unclothed, the tin Sambo was smashed as by a hammer blow. The bedside table and the small cupboard were overturned. And the rocking chair had been pushed into the centre, to preside, tall-backed and erect, like a great brooding bird, over the wreck.

I crossed the room to the window, for perhaps the vandals had gained an entry here. It was tight-bolted and rusted over and the wooden bars were fast and firm. No one had entered here.

As I climbed unsteadily up into Mr Daily's pony trap which waited in the drive, I stumbled and he was obliged to grip my arm and support me until I could regain my strength and I saw that he peered intensely into my face and recognised by its pallor that I had suffered a new shock. But he said nothing about it, only wrapped a heavy rug about my legs, set Spider on my knees for the greater warmth and comfort of us both and then clicked at the pony to turn about.

We left the gravel and went across the rough grass, reached the Nine Lives Causeway and began to traverse it. The tide was dropping back steadily, the sky was a uniform, pearly grey, the air moist and cold but still, after the storm. The marshes lay dull, misty and drear all about us, and, ahead, the flat countryside was dripping and gloomy, without colour, without leaf, without undulation. The pony went steadily and quietly and Mr Daily hummed in a low, tuneless sort of way. I sat as one in a trance, numb, unaware of very much except the movement of the pony trap and the dankness of the air.

But, as we reached the lanes and left the marsh and the estuary behind, I did glance back once over my shoulder. Eel Marsh House stood iron-grey and grim, looming up like a crag, its windows blank and shuttered. There was no sign of any shape or shadow, no living or dead soul. I thought that no one watched us go. Then, the pony's hooves began to clip-clop briskly on the tarmac of the narrow lane between the ditches and straggling blackthorn hedges. I turned my eyes away from that dreadful place for what I fervently prayed was the last time.

From the moment I had climbed into the pony trap, Mr Samuel Daily had treated me as gently and with as much care and concern as an invalid and his efforts to make me feel rested and at ease were redoubled upon arrival at his house. A room had been prepared, a large quiet room with a small balcony overlooking the garden and the open fields beyond. A servant was dispatched at once to the Gifford Arms for the rest of my belongings and, after being given a light breakfast, I was left alone to sleep through the morning. Spider was bathed and groomed and then brought to me, 'since you've got used to her.' And she lay contentedly beside my chair, apparently none the worse for her unpleasant experience early that morning.

I rested but I could not sleep, my brain was still in a confusion and a fever, my nerves all on edge. I was deeply grateful for the peace and tranquillity, but above all for the knowledge that, although I was quite alone and undisturbed here, nevertheless in the house below and the outbuildings beyond there were people, plenty of people, going about their everyday affairs, the reassurance I so badly needed that the normal world still moved through its appointed course.

I tried very hard not to let my mind dwell upon what had happened to me. But I wrote a somewhat guarded letter to Mr Bentley and a fuller one to Stella — though to neither of them did I tell everything nor confess the extent of my distress.

After this, I went outside and took a few turns of the large lawn but the air was cold and raw and I soon returned to my room. There was no sign of Samuel Daily. For an hour or so before noon I dozed fitfully in my chair and, strangely enough, though my body jerked upright once or twice in sudden alarm, after a short time I was able to relax, and so refresh myself more than I would have expected.

At one o'clock there was a knock upon my door and a maid enquired as to whether I would like my luncheon to be served here or if I felt like going down to the dining room.

'Tell Mrs Daily I will join them directly, thank you.'

I washed and tidied myself, called to the dog and walked downstairs.

The Dailys were attentiveness and kindness itself and insistent that I remain with them a day or two longer, before I returned to London. For I had fully decided to go back: nothing on earth would have induced me to pass another hour in Eel Marsh House, I had been as bold and determined as a man could be but I had been defeated and I was not afraid to admit as much, nor did I feel any sense of shame. A man may be accused of cowardice for fleeing away from all manner of physical dangers but when things supernatural, insubstantial and inexplicable threaten not only his safety and well-being but his sanity, his innermost soul, then retreat is not a sign of weakness but the most prudent course.

But I was angry nonetheless, not with myself but with whatever haunted Eel Marsh House, angry at the wild and pointless behaviour of that disturbed creature and angry that it had prevented me, as it would no doubt prevent any other human being, from doing my job. Perhaps I was also angry with those people — Mr Jerome, Keckwick, the landlord, Samuel Daily — who had been proven right about the place. I was young and arrogant enough to feel dashed. I had learned a hard lesson.

That afternoon, left to my own devices again after an excellent luncheon — Mr Daily was soon gone to visit one of his outlying farms — I took out the packet of Mrs Drablow's papers which I had brought with me, for I was still curious about the story I had begun to piece together from my initial reading of the letters and I thought I would divert myself further by trying to complete it. The difficulty was, of course, that I did not know who the young woman — J for Jennet, who had written the letters — was, whether she might have been a relative of Mrs Drablow, or of her husband, or merely a friend. But it seemed most likely that only a blood relation would have given or, rather, been forced to give, her illegitimate child for adoption to another woman, in the way the letters and legal documents revealed.

I felt sorry for J, as I read her short, emotional letters over again. Her passionate love for her child and her isolation with it, her anger and the way she at first fought bitterly against and, finally, gave despairingly into the course proposed to her, filled me with sadness and sympathy. A girl from the servant class, living in a closely-bound community, might perhaps have fared better, sixty or so years before, than this daughter of genteel parentage, who had been so coldly rejected and whose feelings were so totally left out of the count. Yet servant girls in Victorian England had, I knew, often been driven to murder or abandon their misconceived children. At least Jennet had known that her son was alive and had been given a good home.

And then I opened the other documents that were bound together with the letters. They were three death certificates. The first was of the boy, Nathaniel Drablow, at the age of six years. The cause of death was given as drowning. After that, and bearing exactly the same date, was a similar certificate, stating that Rose Judd had also died by drowning.

I felt a terrible, cold, sickening sensation that began in the pit of my stomach and seemed to rise up through my chest into my throat, so that I was sure I would either vomit or choke. But I did not, I only got up and paced in agitation and distress about the room, clutching the two sheets of creased paper in my hand.

After a while, I forced myself to look at the last document also. That too was a death certificate, but dated some twelve years after the other two.

It was for Jennet Eliza Humfrye, spinster, aged thirty-six years. The cause of death was given simply as 'heart failure'.

I sat down heavily in my chair. But I was too agitated to remain there for long and in the end I called to Spider and went out again into the November afternoon that was already closing in to an early twilight, and began to walk, away from Mr Daily's house and garden, past the barns and stables and sheds and off across some stubble. I felt better for the exercise. Around me there was only the countryside, ploughed brown in ridges, with low hedges and, here and there, two or three elm trees, their bare branches full of rooks' nests, from which those ugly black birds flew up in a raucous, flapping flock, every now and then, to reel about, cawing, in the leaden sky. There was a chill wind blowing over the fields driving a spatter of hard rain before it. Spider seemed pleased to be out.

As I walked, my thoughts were all concentrated upon the papers I had just read and the story they had told and which was now becoming clear and complete. I had found out, more or less by chance, the solution — or much of it — to the identity of the woman in black, as well as the answer to many other questions. But, although I now knew more, I was not satisfied by the discovery, only upset and alarmed — and afraid too. I knew — and yet I did not know, I was bewildered and nothing had truly been explained. For how can such things be? I have already stated that I had no more believed in ghosts than does any healthy young man of sound education, reasonable intelligence and matter-of-fact inclinations. But ghosts I had seen. An event, and that a dread-

ful, tragic one, of many years ago, which had taken place and been done with, was somehow taking place over and over again, repeating itself in some dimension other than the normal, present one. A pony and trap, carrying a boy of six called Nathaniel, the adopted son of Mr and Mrs Drablow, and also his nursemaid, had somehow taken a wrong path in the sea mist and veered off the safety of the causeway and on to the marshes, where it had been sucked into the quicksands and swallowed up by the mud and rising waters of the estuary. The child and the nursemaid had been drowned and so presumably had the pony and whoever had been driving the trap. And now, out on those same marshes, the whole episode, or a ghost, a shadow, a memory of it, somehow happened again and again — how often I did not know. But nothing could be seen now, only heard.

The only other things I knew were that the boy's mother, Jennet Humfrye, had died of a wasting disease twelve years after her son, that they were both buried in the now disused and tumble-down graveyard beyond Eel Marsh House; that the child's nursery had been preserved in that house as he had left it, with his bed, his clothes, his toys, all undisturbed, and that his mother haunted the place. Moreover, that the intensity of her grief and distress together with her pent-up hatred and desire for revenge permeated the air all around.

And it was that which so troubled me, the force of those emotions, for those were what I believed had power to harm. But to harm who? Was not everyone connected with that sad story now dead? For presumably Mrs Drablow had been the very last of them.

Eventually I began to be tired and turned back but although I could not find any solution to the business — or perhaps because it was all so inexplicable — I could not put it from my mind, I worried at it all the way home and brooded upon it as I sat in my quiet room, looking out into the evening darkness.

By the time the gong was sounded for dinner I had worked myself up into such a fever of agitation that I determined to pour the whole story out to Mr Samuel Daily and to demand to hear anything whatever that he knew or had ever heard about the business.

The scene was as before, the study of Mr Daily's house after dinner, with the two of us in the comfortable wing chairs, the decanter and glasses between us on the small table. I was feeling considerably better after another good dinner.

I had just come to the end of my story. Mr Daily had sat, listening without interruption, his face turned away from me, as I had relived, though with surprising calm, all the events of my short stay at Eel Marsh House, leading up to the time when he had found me in a faint outside early that morning. And I had also told him of my conclusions, drawn from my perusal of the packet of letters and the death certificates.

He did not speak for some minutes. The clock ticked. The fire burned evenly and sweetly in the grate. The dog Spider lay in front of it on the hearth-rug. Telling the story had been like a purgation and now my head felt curiously light, my body in that limp state such as follows upon a fever or a fright. But I reflected that I could, from this moment on, only get better, because I could only move step by steady step away from those awful happenings, as surely as time went on.

'Well,' he said at last. 'You have come a long way since the night I met you on the late train.'

'It feels like a hundred years ago. I feel like another man.'

'You've gone through some rough seas.'

'Well, I'm in the calm after the storm now and there's an end of it.'

I saw that his face was troubled.

'Come,' I said bravely, 'you don't think any more harm can come of it surely? I never intend to go back there. Nothing would persuade me.'

'No.'

'Then all is well.'

He did not answer, but leaned forward and poured himself another small tot of whisky.

'Though I do wonder what will happen to the house,' I said. 'I'm sure no one local is ever going to want to live there and I can't imagine anyone who might come from outside staying for long, once they get to know what the place is really like — and even if they manage not to hear any of the stories about it in advance. Besides, it's a rambling, inconvenient sort of spot. Whoever would want it?'

Samuel Daily shook his head.

'Do you suppose,' I asked, after a few moments in which we sat in silence with our own thoughts, 'that the poor old woman was haunted night and day by the ghost of her sister and that she had to endure those dreadful noises out there?' — for Mr Daily had told me that the two had been sisters — 'if such was the case, I wonder how she could have endured it without going out of her mind?'

'Perhaps she did not.'

'Perhaps.'

I was growing more and more sensible of the fact that he was holding something back from me, some explanation or information about Eel Marsh House and the Drablow family and, because I knew that, I would not rest or be quite easy in my mind until I had found out everything there was to know. I decided to urge him strongly to tell it to me.

'Was there something I still did not see? If I had stayed there any longer would I have encountered yet more horrors?'

'That I cannot tell.'

'But you could tell me something.'

He sighed and shifted about uneasily in his chair avoiding my eye and looking into the fire, then stretching out his leg to rub at the dog's belly with the toe of his boot.

'Come, we're a good way from the place and my nerves are quite steady again. I must know. It can't hurt me now.'

'Not you,' he said. 'No, not you maybe.'

'For God's sake, what is it you are holding back, man? What are you so afraid of telling me?'

'You, Arthur,' he said, 'will be away from here tomorrow or the next day. You, if you are lucky, will neither hear nor see nor know of anything to do with that damned place again. The rest of us have to stay. We've to live with it.'

'With *what*? Stories — rumours? With the sight of that woman in black from time to time? *With what?*'

'With whatever will surely follow. Sometime or other. Crythin Gifford has lived with that for fifty years. It's changed people. They don't speak of it, you found that out. Those who have suffered worst say least — Jerome, Keckwick.'

I felt my heartbeat increase, I put a hand to my collar to loosen it a little, drew my chair back from the fire. Now that the moment had come, I did not know after all whether I wanted to hear what Daily had to say.

'Jennet Humfrye gave up her child, the boy, to her sister, Alice Drablow, and Alice's husband, because she'd no choice. At first she stayed away — hundreds of miles away — and the boy was brought up a Drablow and was never intended to know his mother. But, in the end, the pain of being parted from him, instead of easing, grew worse and she returned to Crythin. She was not welcome at her parents' house and the man — the child's father — had gone abroad for good. She got rooms in the town. She'd no money. She took in sewing, she acted as a companion to a lady. At first, apparently, Alice Drablow would not let her see the boy at all. But Jennet was so distressed that she threatened violence and in the end the sister relented — just so far. Jennet could visit very occasionally, but never see the boy alone nor ever disclose who she was or that she had any relationship to him. No one ever foresaw that he'd turn out to look so like her, nor that the natural affinity between them would grow out. He became more and more attached to the woman who was, when all was said and done, his own mother, more and more fond, and as he did so, he began to be colder towards Alice Drablow. Jennet planned to take him away, that much I do know. Before she could do so, the accident happened, just as you heard. The boy . . . the nursemaid, the pony trap and its driver Keckwick. . . . '

'*Keckwick?*'

'Yes. His father. And there was the boy's little dog too. That's a treacherous place, as you've found out to your own cost. The sea fret sweeps over the marshes suddenly, the quicksands are hidden.'

'So they all drowned.'

'And Jennet watched. She was at the house, watching from an upper window, waiting for them to return.'

I caught my breath, horrified.

'The bodies were recovered but they left the pony trap, it was held too fast by the mud. From that day Jennet Humfrye began to go mad.'

'Was there any wonder?'

'No. Mad with grief and mad with anger and a desire for revenge. She blamed her sister who had let them go out that day, though it was no one's fault, the mist comes without warning.'

'Out of a clear sky.'

'Whether because of her loss and her madness or what, she also contracted a disease which caused her to begin to waste away. The flesh shrank from her bones, the colour was drained from her, she looked like a walking skeleton — a living spectre. When she went about the streets, people drew back. Children were terrified of her. She died eventually. She died in hatred and misery. And as soon as ever she died the hauntings began. And so they have gone on.'

'What, all the time? Ever since?'

'No. Now and again. Less, these past few years. But still she is seen and the sounds are heard by someone chancing to be out on the marsh.'

'And presumably by old Mrs Drablow?'

'Who knows?'

'Well, Mrs Drablow is dead. There, surely, the whole matter will rest.'

But Mr Daily had not finished. He was just coming to the climax of his story.

'And whenever she has been seen,' he said in a low voice, 'in the graveyard, on the marsh, in the streets of the town, however briefly, and whoever by, there has been one sure and certain result.'

'Yes?' I whispered.

'In some violent or dreadful circumstance, a child has died.'

'What — you mean by accident?'

'Generally in an accident. But once or twice it has been after an illness, which has struck them down within a day or a night or less.'

'You mean any child? A child of the town?'

'Any child. Jerome's child.'

I had a sudden vision of that row of small, solemn faces, with hands all gripping the railings, that surrounded the school yard, on the day of Mrs Drablow's funeral.

'But surely . . . well . . . children sometimes do die.'

'They do.'

'And is there anything more than chance to connect these deaths with the appearance of that woman?'

'You may find it hard to believe. You may doubt it.'

'Well, I . . .'

'We know.'

After a few moments, looking at his set and resolute face, I said quietly, 'I do not doubt, Mr Daily.'

Then, for a very long time, neither of us said anything more.

I knew that I had suffered a considerable shock that morning, after several days and nights of agitation and nervous tension, consequent upon the hauntings of Eel Marsh House. But I did not altogether realise how deeply and badly the whole experience had affected me, both in mind and body.

I went to bed that night, as I supposed for the last time under the Dailys' roof. On the next morning I planned to catch the first available train back to London. When I told Mr Daily of my decision, he did not argue with me.

That night, I slept wretchedly, waking every hour or so out of turbulent nightmares, my entire body in a sweat of anxiety, and when I did not sleep I lay wide awake and tense in every limb, listening, remembering and going over and over it all in my mind. I asked myself unanswerable questions about life and death and the borderlands between and I prayed, direct and simple, passionate prayers.

I had been brought up, like most children, to a belief in the deity, brought up within the Christian church but though I still believed that its teachings were probably the best form of guidance on living a good life, I had found the deity rather remote and my prayers were not anything but formal and dutiful. Not so now. Now, I prayed fervently and with a newly awakened zeal. Now, I realised that there were forces for good and those for evil doing battle together and that a man might range himself on one side or the other.

The morning was long in arriving and, when it did, it was again an overcast and wet one — dank, drear November. I got up, my head aching and eyes burning, my legs heavy, and somehow managed to get dressed and drag myself downstairs to the breakfast table. But I could not face food, though I had an extreme thirst and drank cup after cup of tea. Mr and Mrs Daily glanced at me anxiously now and again, as I talked of my arrangements. I thought that I would not feel well again until I was sitting in the train, watching this countryside slide away out of sight, and I said as much, though at the same time endeavouring to express my great gratitude to them both, because they had indeed been saviours, of my life and of my sanity.

Then I got up from the table and began to make my way to the dining room, but the door receded as I went, I seemed to be fighting towards it through a mist which was closing in upon me, so that I could not get my breath and felt as if I was pushing against a heavy weight which I must remove before I could go any further.

Samuel Daily caught me as I fell and I was dimly aware that, for the second time, though in very different circumstances, he was half-carrying, half-dragging me, this time up the stairs to my bedroom. There, he helped me to undress, there he left me, my head throbbing and my mind confused, and there I remained, having frequent visits from an anxious-looking doctor, for five days. After that, the worst of the fever and the delirium passed, leaving me exhausted and weak beyond belief, and I was able to sit up in an armchair, at first in my room and later downstairs. The Dailys were kindness and solicitude itself. The worst of it all was not the physical illness, the aching, the tiredness, the fever, but the mental turmoil I passed through.

The woman in black seemed to haunt me, even here, to sit on the end of my bed, to push her face suddenly down close to mine as I lay asleep, so I awoke crying out in terror. And my head ran with the sound of the child crying out on the marsh and of the rocking chair and the drowning whinny of the pony. I could not break free of any of them and, when I was not having feverish delusions and nightmares, I was remembering every word of the letters and death certificates, as if I could see the pages held up before my mind's eye.

But at last I began to be better, the fears died down, the visions faded and I found myself again, I was exhausted, drained, but well. There was nothing else the woman could do to me, surely, I had endured and survived.

After twelve days I was feeling almost completely recovered. It was a day of winter sunshine but there had been one of the first frosts of the year. I was sitting at the open French windows of the drawing room, a rug over my knees, looking at the bare bushes and trees, silvery-white and stiff with rime, stark against the sky. It was after lunch. I might sleep a little or not but, in any case, no one would disturb me. Spider lay contentedly at my feet, as she had done throughout the days and nights of my illness. I had grown more fond of the little dog than I would ever have imagined possible, feeling that we shared a bond, because we had been through our time of trial together.

A robin was perched on one of the stone urns at the top of the balustrade, head up, eyes bead-bright, and I watched him happily, while he hopped a foot or two and then paused again, to listen and to sing. I reflected that, before coming here, I would never have been able to concentrate on such an ordinary thing so completely but would have been restless to be up and off, doing this or that busily. Now, I appreciated the bird's presence, enjoyed simply watching his movements for as long as he chose to remain outside my window, with an intensity I had never before experienced.

I heard some sounds outside, the engine of a motor car, voices round at the front of the house, but paid them little attention, so wrapped up was I in my observation of the bird. Besides, they would have nothing to do with me.

There were footsteps along the corridor and they stopped outside the door of the drawing room, and then after a hesitation it opened. Perhaps it was later than I thought, and someone had come to see how I was and whether I wanted a cup of tea.

'Arthur?'

I turned, startled, and then jumped from my chair in amazement, disbelief, and delight. Stella, my own dear Stella, was coming towards me across the room.

The Woman in Black

THE FOLLOWING MORNING, I left the house. We were taken, in Mr Samuel Daily's motor, directly to the railway station. I had settled my account at the Gifford Arms by messenger, and I did not go into the town of Crythin Gifford again; it seemed altogether wise to take medical advice, for the doctor had been particularly anxious that I should not do anything, or go anywhere, to upset my still delicately balanced equilibrium. And, in truth, I did not *want* to see the town, or to risk meeting Mr Jerome or Keckwick, or, most of all, to catch so much as a glimpse of the distant marsh. All that was behind me, it might have happened, I thought, to another person. The doctor had told me to put the whole thing from my mind, and I resolved to try and do so. With Stella beside me, I did not see how I could fail.

The only regret I had at leaving the place was a genuine sadness at parting company with Mr and Mrs Samuel Daily, and, when we shook hands, I made him promise that he would visit us, when he next came to London — which he did, he said, once or, at most, twice a year. Moreover, a puppy was booked for us, as soon as Spider should produce any. I was going to miss the little dog a great deal.

But there was one last question I had to ask, though I found it hard to bring the matter up.

'I must know,' I burst out at last, while Stella was safely out of earshot and deep in conversation with Mrs Daily, whom she had been able to draw out, with her own natural friendliness and warmth.

Samuel Daily looked at me sharply.

'You told me that night —' I took a deep breath to try and calm myself. 'A child — a child in Crythin Gifford has always died.'

'Yes.'

I could not go on but my expression was enough, I knew, my desperate anxiety to be told the truth was evident.

'Nothing,' Daily said quickly. 'Nothing has happened. . .'

I was sure he had been going to add 'Yet', but he stopped and so I added it for him. But he only shook his head silently.

'Oh, pray God it may not — that the chain is broken — that her power is at an end — that she has gone — and I was the last ever to see her.'

He put a hand reassuringly on my arm. 'Yes, yes.'

I wanted above all for it to be so, for the time that had elapsed since I had last seen the woman in black — the ghost of Jennet Humfrye — to be long enough now, for it to be proof positive that the curse had quite gone. She had been a poor, crazed, troubled woman, dead of grief and distress, filled with hatred and desire for revenge. Her bitterness was understandable, the wickedness that led her to take away another woman's children because she had lost her own, understandable too but not forgivable.

There was nothing anyone could do to help her, except perhaps pray for her soul, I thought. Mrs Drablow, the sister she blamed for the death of her child, was dead herself and in her grave, and, now that the house was empty at last, perhaps the hauntings and their terrible consequences for the innocent would cease forever.

The car was waiting in the drive. I shook hands with the Dailys and, taking Stella's arm and keeping tightly hold of it, climbed in and leaned back against the seat. With a sigh — indeed almost a sob — of relief, I was driven away from Crythin Gifford.

133

My story is almost done. There is only the last thing left to tell. And that I can scarcely bring myself to write about. I have sat here at my desk, day after day, night after night, a blank sheet of paper before me, unable to lift my pen, trembling and weeping too. I have gone out and walked in the old orchard and further, across the country beyond Monk's Piece, for mile after mile, but seen nothing of my surroundings, noticing neither animal nor bird, unable to tell even the state of the weather, so that several times I have come home soaked through to the skin, to Esmé's considerable distress. And that has been another cause of anguish: she has watched me and wondered and been too sensitive to ask questions, I have seen the worry and distress on her face and sensed her restlessness, as we have sat together in the late evenings. I have been quite unable to tell her anything at all, she has no idea what I have been going through or why: she will have no idea until she reads this manuscript and at that time I shall be dead and beyond her.

But, now at last, I have summoned up sufficient courage, I will use the very last of my strength, that has been so depleted by the reliving of those past horrors, to write the end of the story.

Stella and I returned to London and within six weeks we had married. Our original plan had been to wait at least until the following spring but my experiences had changed me greatly, so that I now had an urgent sense of time, a certainty that we should not delay, but seize upon any joy, any good fortune, any opportunity, at once, and hold fast to it. Why should we wait? What was there beyond the mundane considerations of money, property and possessions to keep us from marrying? Nothing. And so we married, quietly and without fuss, and lived in my old rooms, with another room added, which the landlady had been more than willing to rent to us, until such time as we could afford a small house of our own. We were as happy as a young man and his bride may possibly be, content in each other's company, not rich but not poor either, busy and looking forward to the future. Mr Bentley gave me a little more responsibility and a consequent increase in salary as time went on. About Eel Marsh House and the Drablow estate and papers I had expressly begged him that I be told nothing and so I was not; the names were never mentioned to me again.

A little over a year after our marriage, Stella gave birth to our child, a son, whom we called Joseph Arthur Samuel, and Mr Samuel Daily was his godfather, for he was our sole remaining tie with that place, that time. But, although we saw him occasionally in London, he never once spoke of the past; indeed, I was so filled with joy and contentment in my life, that I never so much as thought of those things, and the nightmares quite ceased to trouble me.

I was in a particularly peaceful, happy frame of mind one Sunday afternoon in the summer of the year following our son's birth. I could not have been less prepared for what was to come.

We had gone to a large park, ten miles or so outside London, which formed the grounds of a noble house and, in the summer season, stood open to the general public at weekends. There was a festive, holiday air about the place, a lake, on which small boats were being rowed, a bandstand, with a band playing jolly tunes, stalls selling ices and fruit. Families strolled in the sunshine, children tumbled about upon the grass. Stella and I walked happily, with young Joseph taking a few unsteady steps, holding onto our hands while we watched him, as proud as any parents could be.

Then, Stella noticed that one of the attractions upon offer was a donkey, and a pony and trap, on both of which rides could be taken, down an avenue of great horse-chestnut trees, and, thinking that the boy would find such a treat to his liking, we led him to the docile grey donkey and I endeavoured to lift him up into the saddle. But he shrieked and pulled away at once, and clung to me, while at the same time pointing to the pony trap, and gesturing excitedly. So, because there was only room for two passengers, Stella took Joseph, and I stood, watching them bowl merrily away down the ride, between the handsome old trees, which were in full, glorious leaf.

For a while, they went out of sight, away round a bend, and I began to look idly about me, at the other enjoyers of the afternoon. And then, quite suddenly, I saw her. She was standing away from any of the people, close up to the trunk of one of the trees.

I looked directly at her and she at me. There was no mistake. My eyes were not deceiving me. It was she, the woman in black with the wasted face, the ghost of Jennet Humfrye. For a second, I simply stared in incredulity and astonishment, then in cold fear.

I was paralysed, rooted to the spot on which I stood, and all the world went dark around me and the shouts and happy cries of all the children faded. I was quite unable to take my eyes away from her. There was no expression on her face and yet I felt all over again the renewed power emanating from her, the malevolence and hatred and passionate bitterness. It pierced me through.

At that same moment, to my intense relief, the pony cart came trotting back down the avenue, through the shafts of sunlight that lay across the grass, with my dear Stella sitting in it and holding up the baby, who was bouncing and calling and waving his little arms with delight. They were almost back, they had almost reached me, I would retrieve them and then we would go, for I didn't

want to stay here for a second longer. I made ready. They had almost come to a halt when they passed the tree beside which the woman in black was still standing and, as they did so, she moved quickly, her skirts rustling as if to step into the pony's path. The animal swerved violently and then reared a little, its eyes filled with sudden fright, and then it took off and went careering away through the glade between the trees, whinnying and quite out of control. There was a moment of dreadful confusion, with several people starting off after it, and women and children shrieking. I began to run crazily and then I heard it, the sickening crack and thud as the pony and its cart collided with one of the huge tree trunks. And then silence — a terrible silence which can only have

lasted for seconds, and seemed to last for years. As I raced towards where it had fallen, I glanced back over my shoulder. The woman had disappeared.

They lifted Stella gently from the cart. Her body was broken, her neck and legs fractured, though she was still conscious. The pony had only stunned itself but the cart was overturned and its harness tangled, so that it could not move, but lay on the ground whinnying and snorting in fright.

Our baby son had been thrown clear, clear against another tree. He lay crumpled on the grass below it, dead.

This time, there was no merciful loss of consciousness, I was forced to live through it all, every minute and then every day thereafter, for ten long months, until Stella, too, died from her terrible injuries.

I had seen the ghost of Jennet Humfrye and she had had her revenge.

They asked for my story. I have told it. Enough.